THE RETURN OF FRANKENSTEIN

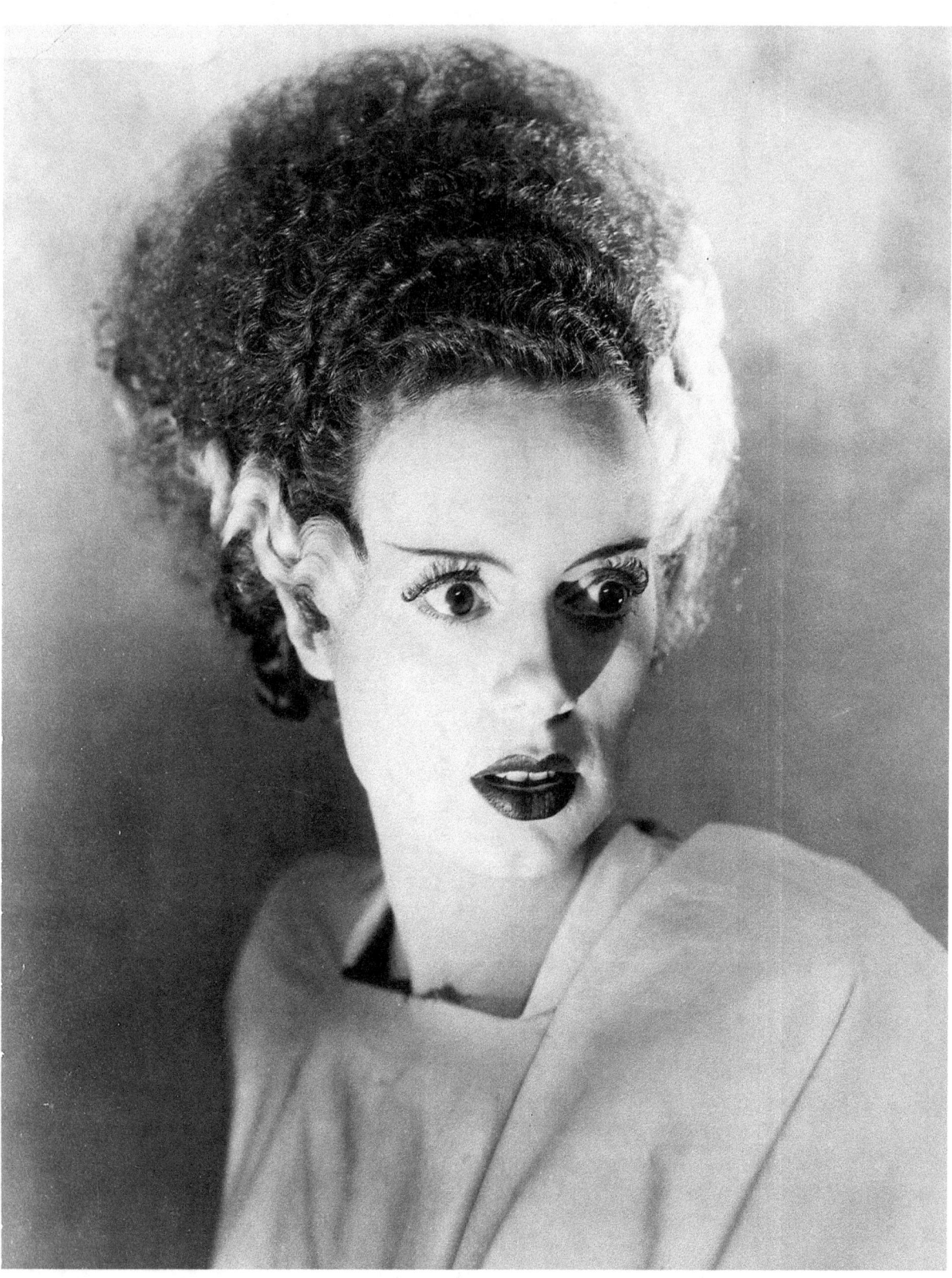

Books by
Philip J Riley

CLASSIC HORROR FILMS
Frankenstein, the original 1931 shooting script
Bride of Frankenstein, the original 1935 shooting script
Son of Frankenstein, the original 1939 shooting script
Ghost of Frankenstein, the original 1942 shooting script
Frankenstein Meets the Wolf Man, the original 1943 shooting script
House of Frankenstein, the original 1944 shooting script
The Mummy, the original 1932 shooting script
The Mummy's Curse the original 1944 shooting script (as Editor in Chief)
The Wolf Man, the original 1941 shooting script
Dracula, the original 1931 shooting script
House of Dracula, the original 1945 shooting script

CLASSIC COMEDY FILMS
Abbott & Costello Meet Frankenstein, the original 1948 shooting script

CLASSIC SCIENCE FICTION
This Island Earth, the original 1955 shooting script
The Creature from the Black Lagoon, the original 1953 shooting script (editor-in-chief)

THE ACKERMAN ARCHIVES SERIES - LOST FILMS
The Reconstruction of London After Midnight, the original 1927 shooting script
The Reconstruction of A Blind Bargain, the original 1922 shooting script
The Reconstruction of The Hunchback of Notre Dame, the original 1923 shooting script

CLASSIC SILENT FILMS
The Reconstruction of The Phantom of the Opera, the original 1925 shooting script
The Reconstruction of "London After Midnight" the original 1927 hooting script (2nd edition)
The Divine Woman 1928 by Gladys Unger (Editor)

FILMONSTER SERIES - LOST SCRIPTS
James Whale's Dracula's Daughter, 1934
Cagliostro, The King of the Dead, 1932
Wolf Man vs. Dracula 1944
Lon Chaney as Dracula/Nosferatu
Robert Florey's Frankenstein 1931
Frankenstein - A play, 1931 (editor)
War Eagles (as editor)
Karloff as The Invisible Man 1932
Lon Chaney, as The Man Who Laughs, 1924
The Return of Frankenstein 1934

AS EDITOR
Countess Dracula by Carroll Borland
My Hollywood, when both of us were young by Patsy Ruth Miller
Mr. Technicolor - Herbert Kalmus
Famous Monster of Filmland #2 by Forrest J Ackerman
The Wizard of MGM by A. Arnold Gillespie - co-editor with Robert Welch
BearManormedia's NightMare Series

FILM DOCUMENTARIES
A Thousand Faces - as contributor (Photoplay Productions)
Universal Horrors - as contributor (Photoplay Productions)

Mr. Riley has also contributed to 12 film related books by various authors as well as numerous magazine articles and received the Count Dracula Society Awar and was inducted into Universal's Horror Hall of Fame adn won a Halloween Book Festival 2011 & 2012 award in the horror catagory

Publicity photograph of Boris Karloff in 1935

THE RETURN
OF
FRANKENSTEIN

An Alternate History for Classic Film Monsters
Script by John L. Balderston

By

Philip J. Riley

Hollywood Publishing Archives

BearManor Media

BearManor Media
P.O. Box 1129
Duncan, OK 73534-1129

Phone: 580-252-3547
Fax: 814-690-1559

www.bearmanormedia.com

The Author would like to thank the following individuals who contributed and helped make
this series possible. Carl Laemmle Jr., R.C.Sherriff, Stanley Bergerman, Gloria Holden, Jane
Wyatt, Otto Kruger, Marcel Delgado, Robert Florey, Paul Ivano (Cinematographer), Paul
Malvern (producer), Elsa Lanchester, Merion C. Cooper, Patric Leroux, Bette Davis, Bela G.
Lugosi, Technicolor Corporation, John Balderston III, Loeb and Loeb Attorneys, David Stanley
Horsley ASC, Sara Karloff, John Teehan, George Turner, Al Magliochetti

Author's Note: I interviewed the producers, directors, stars, cast and crew in the early to late
1970s. They were recalling events that happened 35-45 years previous and sometimes memory
fades or events are recalled from their perspective point of view.

First Edition
10 9 8 7 6 5 4 3 2 1

The purpose of this series is the preservation of the art of writing for the screen. Rare books
have long been a source of enjoyment and an investment for the serious collector, and even in
limited editions there are thousands printed. Scripts, however, numbered only 50 at the most.
In the history of American Literature, the screenwriter was being lost in time. It is my hope that
my efforts bring about a renewed history and preservation of a great American Literary form,
The Screenplay, by preserving them for study by future generations.

Recommended reading: *Hollywood Gothic* by David Skal, 1990, WW Norton & Company;
James Whale a new world of Gods and Monsters University of Minnesota Press 1998 edition by
James Curtis; *City of Dreams* by Bernard F. Dick, 1997 University of Kentucky: *James Whale A
Biography or The Would-be Gentleman* by Mark Gatiss, Cassell Wellington House 1995; Excerpts
from R. C. Sherriff's *No Leading Ladies* (London: Golancz 1968)

THE RETURN OF FRANKENSTEIN

A scene cut from the final release print - The Monster kidnaps Elizabeth to force Frankenstein to make him a mate.
The kidnaping of Elizabeth takes place in the film - but this scene was considered to lurid by the censors

January 5, 1935 - UNIVERSAL WEEKLY

JAMES WHALE put "The Return of Franken-stein" into work at Universal City Wednesday with almost the entire cast in attendance. Karloff will be starred, and in a make-up which requires from six to seven hours to put on. Valerie Hobson, whose work in "The Mystery of Edwin Drood," has made her an outstanding figure at Universal City, has the feminine lead.

Colin Clive will play the part of Frankenstein, as in the original, and Ernest Thesiger, who was in "The Old Dark House" for Universal, O.P. Heggie, E.E. Clive and Una O'Connor, all favorite James Whale players, have important parts.

James Whale feels that he has made an extremely happy choice to fill the role of the bride of Franken-stein. A number of European and American actresses and screen players were tried out and considered for the role. Among them were Bridgitte Helm and Phyllis Brooks. The requirement was the quintessence of cold beauty. Elsa Lanchester, who played Ann of Cleves in "The Private Life of Henry the Eighth was finally suggested, and her tests won her the role, hands down.

When the sequel to "Frankenstein" was first projected, the title, "The Bride of Frankenstein," was used, but since the monster is not named Franken-stein, this title was given up in favor of "The Return of Frankenstein" The story was written by John L. Balderston, who adapted "Frankenstein" and the screenplay was made by Edmund Pearson, noted author of mystery stories, and William Hurlbut.

Charles Laughton and his wife, Elsa Lanchester, who was set to be
"The Monster's Mate" even in the early screenplays

Edward Van Sloan was to play Father Gerard

Dwight Frye

Colin Clive

Mae Clarke, who was said to have dropped out due to illness

Valerie Hobson who replaced Mae Clarke as Elizabeth

The final cut of *Frankenstein* as it exists today shows that Universal considered making a sequel as early as its 1931 preview screenings, following which the film's original ending was changed to allow for Henry Frankenstein's survival. Whale, who was Carl Laemmle Jr.'s choice to direct, stalled and took advantage of the situation in persuading the studio to let him make *One More River* a tactic he would us for 3 more years to avoid making the film.

"*The New Adventures of Frankenstein (The Monster Lives!)*, a treatment by a *Frankenstein* scenarist, Robert Florey, was rejected in February of 1932 by the youthful studio chief, Carl Laemmle, Jr.

Universal staff writer Tom Reed wrote a treatment under the title *The Return of Frankenstein*, a title retained until filming began. Following its acceptance in 1933, Reed wrote a full script that was submitted to the Hays office for review. The script passed its review but Whale, who by then had been put under contract by the Laemmles to direct, rejected the script. L. G. Blochman and Philip MacDonald (Treatments included in this book) were the next writers assigned, but Whale also found their work unsatisfactory. The writers contocted some interesting stories. In one treatment they had Frankenstein taping into New York City's main electric power source to generate the power to create the monster's mate. Another had Frankenstein hiding out in a Gypsy caravan to avoid being caught and put on trial for the murders the monster had committed.

In 1934, Laemmle Jr. set John L. Balderston to work on yet another version, and it was he who returned to an incident from the novel in which the creature demands a mate. In the novel Frankenstein creates a mate, but destroys it without bringing it to life. Balderston also created the Mary Shelley, Percy Shelley and Lord Byron prologue. (As you will see Balderston had every right to lodge a complaint to Universal and challenge them as to the authorship credits for the final shooting script which was submitted for Hays office review in November 1934). This is the script that Whale used to start his production but after several months Whale was still not satisfied with Balderston's work and handed the project to playwright William J. Hurlbut and Edmund Pearson. This shooting script can be seen in the MagicImage Filmbooks volume 2 "Bride of Frankenstein (1989) and shows us today just how much Whale added and by doing so, creating what most Classic Monster Film fans consider the best of the Universal 1930's productions.

From the January, 1998, American Cinematographer Magazine an article by Jan A Henderson and George E. Turner stated:

"In 1933, director Kurt Neumann, a Laemmle protege from Germany, was put in charge of developing the project for Karloff and Bela Lugosi.

"Whale would eventually relent, however. By early 1934, having made six successful movies (*The Impatient Maiden, The Old Dark House, The Kiss Before the Mirror, The Invisible Man, By Candlelight* and *One More River*) the director had a change of heart. Assisted by R.C. Sherriff, he began preparing the *Frankenstein* sequel from scratch. Sherriff became homesick, and soon returned to Oxford, (England). Whale then worked with Balderston and William Hurlbut, author of the play *Lillies of the Field*. Whale began casting the picture while the script was being written, and had alterations made to accomodate his actors of choice. Balderston angrily demanded that his name be removed from the screenplay, but was still given credit (with Hurlbut) for the adaptation.

"The script met with severe opposition from Joseph Breen, administrator of the Production Code. Whale wrote a solicitous letter assuring him that any depiction of necrophilia, gruesomeness and religious images would be modified to suit the demands of the Code."

The other informative article is published on Wikipedia and has these interesting reactions to the final release print of *Bride of Frankenstein*

"Following its release with the Code seal of approval, the film was challenged by the censorship board in the state of Ohio. Censors in England and China objected to the scene in which the Monster gazes longingly upon the as yet unanimated body of the Bride, citing concerns that it looked like necrophilia. Universal voluntarily withdrew the film from Sweden because of the extensive cuts demanded, and *Bride* was rejected outright by Trinidad, Palestine and Hungary. One unusual objection, from Japanese censors, was that the scene in which Pretorius chases his miniature Henry VIII with tweezers constituted "making a fool out of a king"."

The script that you will be reading in this volume is the final approved script by John L. Balderston, before any changes were made by Whale and Hurlbut.

Ernest Thesiger (Left) , who was not in the original script - but added when James Whale finally agreed to make the picture (Below) - another cut scene from the final film - E.E. Clive, as the Burgomaster, in chair

(Above - Karl goes on a murderous rampage and blames the monster. (Below) The little girl murdered - not shown in final release.

The Monster gathers wood for the family in whose home he is hiding and learning to speak.

14

(Above) *The bodies keep piling up* - *(Below -a publicity shot)*

James Whale (right) directing Boris Karloff, Cinematographer John Mescall - far right

John L. Balderston, Author, Screenwriter, playwright
(Oct. 22, 1889–March 8, 1954)

William James Hurlbut
July 13, 1878–May 4, 1957

"THE RETURN OF FRANKENSTEIN"

BY

PHILIP MAC DONALD

December 26, 1933

THE RETURN OF FRANKENSTEIN

ORIGINAL STORY
BY

Philip MacDonald

The screen is filled by the upper half of the front page of
a newspaper in German. Startling headlines refer to the
imminence of war and the necessity for stopping war. The newspaper fades and is replaced by another, in French. The headlines are practically the same. This process is repeated very
quickly with other languages and then becomes English. Enough
of the paper can be seen to establish the fact that war between
two small middle-European states is imminent; it must be
stopped or this will be the beginning of another world wide
conflagration such as that of 1914......

The sound of an express train is heard while the
paper is on the screen. It swells in volume, and the train
itself crashes through the paper.

It is a transcontinental flyer. We come to the interior of a special car attached to the train. It is the car
of a delegation from the League of Nations. All the major
countries are represented. Listening to the conversation, we
discover that the Delegation is on its way to the town of
Goldstadt. It is to visit Dr. Frankenstein. It becomes clear
that Frankenstein has perfected what he refers to as the Delta
ray, and has offered this, under certain conditions, to the
League. Some members of the Delegation frankly scoff, but
others are hopeful, saying that Frankenstein's discovery will
be such as to empower its possessors to prohibit war. One

of the hopeful delegates bases his faith upon the fact that
Frankenstein is infinitely ahead of any other scientist and,
having this statement challenged, he even refers to queer
stories which circulated some years before concerning a previous experiment of Frankenstein's........

Leaving the Delegation, we come to the interior of
a sick room in Goldstadt's leading hospital. In bed is
Elizabeth Frankenstein. Visiting her is Victor Moritz, who
has been as was shown in the first story of Frankenstein)
always in love with her since boyhood. Elizabeth, though able
to talk, is very ill and it is possible that she may have to
be operated upon. Her condition is responsive to Victor's
attitude being more only that that one who loves her than he
normally permits himself. They talk. Elizabeth weakly asks
whether Victor has seen her husband. Victor, trying to conceal
his anger with his friend for omitting to visit the hospital,
explains that today Henry is receiving the League Delegation.
From Elizabeth's reaction to this we gather that she is
deeply concerned about her husband's experiments: she feels
that nothing but ill can come of them: once before he
penetrated regions into which man should not delve, and misery
came of that. What will happen now, Victor tries to soothe
her - and we leave the pair.

We come now to Frankenstein's house at the very edge
of the town. At one side of the house is his laboratory. The
Delegation are being admitted to the house. They are told that
Dr. Frankenstein is in his laboratory and will be with them
in a few minutes. While they wait in the drawing room we first

see Frankenstein's son, a boy of two.

In the laboratory. This is a huge chamber, two uninterrupted stories in height and vast in floor space. There are here, of course, all the ordinary appurtenances of a scientist's work-place but there are also - and the majority of the space - given up to these - all the strange appliances which govern the delta ray. In the center of the laboratory, resting upon a huge shaft which controls its height and is now at about six feet from the ground, is a vast box of gleaming metal which is the Projector of the ray. Along one wall is the control board of the ray - gauges, figures dials, control-wheels, and the like. Two men are in the laboratory. Frankenstein and his chief assistant Kurt. They are similarly and curiously clad, in tight-fitting, enveloping garments of a curious grey, faintly gleaming materials. They wear gloves over their hands and upon a table are two head-pieces which are of the same genre as the most modern gas masks. Kurt is placing a long table of chromium steel before the Projector. This task finished, the Delegation is admitted. Frankenstein greets them and they look about them with the faintly awed curiosity of laymen.

Frankenstein asks whether they are ready for the test and the leader of the Delegation assents; but, remarking upon Frankenstein's garb, assumes that it is protective and asks whether there is danger. Frankenstein smiles grimly and says: "Not for you - you will all sit here, behind." He arranges chairs - all of chromium steel like the other fittings in the laboratory - behind the great Projector.

He and his assistant then put on their masks - and become
de-humanized. They seem, now, more like the Martians of a
dream than men. But the subjects of the test, which they now
arrange upon the steel table before the Projector, are
definitely of this world - a little steel cage with a bright-
eyes, sleek guinea pig lying down within it; a crystal bowl
filled with clear water in which are darting about the lithe,
auriferous shapes of two gold fish; a pot of steel filled with
dark rich loam from which there rise, in tall and graceful
shapes, green, delicate, growing ferns.

Frankenstein raises the visor of his mask. He
looks grimly at the assembled delegates now seated in line
like so man wondering children. He says: "Are you ready,
gentlemen? Do not upon any account move from where you are
sitting." He lowers the visor of his mask, and going to the
control board, turns the biggest of the several wheels, while
the great box of the Projector tilts until it is directly in
line with the objects upon the table.

His assistant is at the control board too, and to
him Frankenstein, his voice muffled by the mask, gives orders.
The assistant turns a switch and immediately there begins a
giant humming sound which makes all the watchers start in
their seats. It is the hum of the great generator.
Frankenstein shouts at his assistant, who moves from the
generator switch to a little panel of buttons. He presses
four of these and steel blinds come down over all the great
windows, and the scene is suddenly dark. A murmur of excited,
apprehensive talk comes from the members of the Delegation

and then dies away. Again we hear an order from Frankenstein
and suddenly, from the Projector there shines a streak of
curious light; neither white nor coloured, but a sort of a
grayish effulgence which is not so much light as a lessening
of darkness. It is the only light in the great chamber. By
it are thrown into relief the bowl and the cage and the fern
pot. For an instant we see no change - and then we become aware
that the fern-fonds are drooping and withering before our
eyes; that the guinea pig has rolled over onto its side; that
the fish are still.... The fern is black and wilted; the
little animal is limp and dead and blackening; the fish, dis-
coloured and seeming half their former size, are floating
upon the top of the water.....

Shouted orders from Frankenstein. Activity at the
control board. The hum of the great generator ceases, leaving
deathly silence; the steel blinds fly up with a clang and once
more the light of day shines into the place...... Frankenstein
takes off his mask. He walks to the shaken members of his
audience. The ray is off. He, beckons them and, gingerly,
one by one, they come forward. Frankenstein does not speak,
but he points to things upon the table and the visitors
crowd round it.

The leader of the Delegation draws Frankenstein
aside. Frankenstein says: "You've seen. Do you accept my
offer? The leader, being a diplomatist, is horrified at
such bluntness. He says, in effect, that he and his
colleagues have seen and have been much impressed. But -

they want to know more. Frankenstein, in curt phrases, says
that they seem to have misunderstood his communication. He
has discovered this force and he is not taking the risk of
disclosing its secret, without terms. He is a rich man; he
does not need money; he will supply the secret to the major
powers of the world in order that they may have a superlative
power to keep peace; but he will not supply it in such a way
that any one power may achieve it's ownership. In brief, all
can have it or none. Do they want it? The leader of the
Delegation says that he must confer. Could Herr Frankenstein
give them an hour. "I will give you all day. Now I am busy,
I must go. Come and see me tonight." And with this he is
gone, leaving behind him extreme agitation. Diplomats are
not used to being treated in this way......

We follow Frankenstein. We see him find his son
and take the boy with him, telling the child that they are
going to see Elizabeth......

Now the hospital. Elizabeth and Victor. Victor's
concern has at last lead him to a reassertion of the love which
he has not mentioned for many years. We see Elizabeth's
reaction to this and find, that hopelessly, she returns is
love; but we realize that they both accept the situation as
it is. We then come to Frankenstein and his infant son. They
are entering the room and Frankenstein has heard enough at
least to show him that Victor reels more than friendship for
Elizabeth. He comes in, with the child, and after a few
moments Victor goes. After greeting the boy, Elizabeth sets

him to playing by himself while she talks in low tones with
her husband. She endeavors, desperately, to dissuade him
from further traffic with his discovery. She tells him,
forcibly, that he has play with Life and made misery and that
he is now playing with Death and will make more misery; that
he is, in fact, dabblling with Forbidden Things. Gently the
almost fanatical Frankenstein repels her pleading, his answer
being that he is not making Death, but an enforcer of Peace;
in the way in which he will give his discovery to the world,
it will mean the end of war...... But he cannot convince
Elizabeth.

Once more in Frankenstein's house the Delegation
have added to their number the Prime Minister of the Country.
They await Frankenstein. From their talk we learn that the
Prime Minister has assented to some proposal. The Delegation
has decided that they want a test upon the grand scale and
the Prime Minister has hit upon a way in which this can be done
if Frankenstein will consent. Frankenstein's house and
laboratory face a practicaally unpopulated stretch of country
which comprises rough pasture land, foothills, and then
beyond, the mountains themselves. It is the Government's
intention to draw a path about twenty miles in length and
about two hundred yards wide in a straight line from the
laboratory into the mountains. It will be their responsibility
to see that all mountaineers, farmers and such keep themselves
and their cattle off this strip during the period of the
test. Frankenstein, consents immediately. The Prime

Minister states that he will make the necessary arrangements
at once. He goes, and the Delegation then clusters round
Frankenstein. They want to know more about the ray.
Sardonically he repeats his determination not to tell anyone
about it. But at last he tells them generalities which will
not disclose the secret. He explains shortly that what he has
christened the Delta ray is of enormously negative electric
power. Every man of education must know that all life contains
electrons or positive electricity. The Delta ray, being so
intensely negative attracts to it - back to its generator -
all positive electrons. All forms of life, without their
positive electrons, are thrown out of 'balance' and necessarily
wither and die... More questions are asked, but Frankenstein
harshly refuses answers. With an injunction to wait until
tomorrow and the test he shows the Delegation out - and we
fade to -

The next day. Activity throughout Government
offices in Goldstadt and parts of the countryside, as the
Government put their scheme into operation. We see varying
shots of the effects of this activity: the pressure under
which the organizers are working in the city; a regiment of
cavalry riding along the prescribed path and marking it off
with danger flags; Burgomasters of small country and mountain
communities receiving telephoned instructions and passing
them on to the gendarmerie and villagers; cattle-driving
parties; bodies of men fencing off certain sections of the
path; and so on and so on. We concentrate at last upon a
fencing group; right in the mountains. They are peasants,

under the direction of a young sergeant of the military.
From fragments of talk we learn that they are mostly tenants
of the Barony of Frankenstein. The camera moves and we see
that one croup is working near some blackened ruins - a great
heap of charred embers, crumbled and rotting plaster, skeleton
arms of what must once have been windmill-sails and all the
other rotting debris of a building long since destroyed by fire.
Atop of the debris, roughly in the shape of a cross, are
lying two huge charred beams of oak. Moving this way and that
among the group we hear vague references to the 'burning of
the mill,' and then we center upon one member of the group,
who by his actions, voice and perpetual, wild stare is plainly
not mentally as other men are. (Anyone who has seen the first
picture of Frankenstein will recognize the peasant whose
little daughter was killed by the Monster). The Sergeant in
charge of the fencing party strolls up to this group. The
wild-eyed, half-crazed peasant is talking. He is pointing to
the mill ruins; his eyes and crazed imagination have been
caught by the crucifix-like arrangement of the two beams.
His talk makes no sense to the young Sergeant, who whispers
a question to another member of the group. The questioner
is amazed that the Sergeant does not know the history of
those ruins and briefly, in simple and trenchant words, tells
of the four-year-old tragedy - of the Thing, which some men
still say was created by the young Baron Frankenstein, and
which killed a child and tried to kill its maker and was at
last burned to death! "Somewhere under there!" says the old
peasant, stabbing a forefinger, 'is what is left of the

Thing......' The sergeant, an unimaginative young soldier,
shrugs the story off as mountaineer's superstition. Laughing
he strolls away, but the old man's words have aroused
memories in his fellows, and it is with furtive sidelong
glances at the pile or ruins that they go on with their work
in silence.....

Back in Frankenstein's house in Goldstadt. Night.
Henry Frankenstein is receiving, over the telephone, the ALL-
Clear. He summons his assistant to his laboratory - and the
great test begins. While in the laboratory the three curiously
clad figures flit about their work under the glare of powerful lights - making calculations, altering the position of the
great Projector, checking their calculations by map and
electric compass - we see that outside the long windows
darkness has fallen....

All is ready. Frankenstein himself switches on
the giant generator. Again the titanic hum assualts the ear
and we see the gray light start out from the huge steel box
of the Projector.

Outside we slowly follow the creeping light of the
ray as it cuts a swathe through the darkness of the desolate
country, not only slaying the darkness but leaving behind it,
as it creeps onwards, a path of death......grass withers and
is black. The foliage of trees droops, and the trees themselves wilt almost humanly and fall slowly to the ground....
The ray goes on. It reaches the foothills.... It passes
them.... A goat strayed from some careless herder's flock

blunders out of the darkness and into the deadly grey light
and checks, sways, stumbles and falls lifeless ....The
ray goes on. It seems to delve into the side of a mountain
and ceases, but seems to delve into the side of a mountain
and cease, but as the camera rounds the great mass of rock
we see that the ray, uninterrupted, is springing from the
far side and continuing its slow and deadly way ..... We
see more; we see that now it has reached the ruins of the
old mill. They lie directly in the middle of its path. It
touches them and goes on. Following it, we wonder whether
we indeed saw the beam which makes the cross piece of the
crucifix shape move, or whether it was some trick of the
queer light..... Back in the Laboratory Frankenstein is
watching his two assistants manipulate the controls. He is
looking at his watch. He says: 'Now! Up fifty, for five
minutes.' And watching the men at the board in a close shot
we see that one of them turns a central small wheel over
which is a needle-armed dial: the pointer on the dial has
been standing at five hundred, but now it flickers up to
five hundred and fifty.

Again we are out on the dark mountainside; but
now the light of the ray is brighter. The ruins of the
mill are in the foreground of the picture and, as we watch,
we realize that we did see the topmost beam move! For now
its movement is obvious. One end of it is rising, not
steadily but jerkily and continuously. It seems that it
must be actuated by some force beneath it.... It attains the
perpendicular and falls with a soft crash the other way!
And then the second beam moves more quickly. It does not
rise but rolls - and over one charred edge of it we see

something move.......

The camera goes closer: the moving thing is a frightful travesty of human arm. It is flecked white and black, the white being islands of unharmed flesh surrounded by the blackness of burning.....

Again our viewpoint changes; to one further away. The rotting debris beneath the second beam seems imbued with life. It is moving. Charred smouldering fragments roll here and there with little hissing sounds and then something - slowly - rises to the full of a giant height. Mercifully, we cannot, in the queer light of the ray, see very clearly. But we see enough. We see the half-burnt, half-mouldered form of the Monster ..... It stands for a moment, swaying. It leans in the full light of the ray, towards the direction from which the ray is coming. It moves, stiffly, dreadful arms - and one of these arms covers its face .... It moves. It makes a jerky little dash, its arms still covering its ravaged head, towards the side of the ray. It is obvious that it is trying to escape. But it cannot! It is drawn irresistibly along the path of the ray, back towards the ray's inception ......

The laboratory again. Frankenstein is looking at his watch. He says: "We'll try it full strength for five minutes; and then cut. Put her up to a thousand!"

The mountains again. The ray suddenly increases its light. For in the background, but stumbling forward, towards the camera, we see the Monster. With the increased force of the ray it is now moving with nearly twice the

speed that it had before. As it goes, strangled cries come
from it. It is plain that it is still - with what volition
it possesses - trying to get away from the ray. But it
cannot; it is borne onwards. Obstacles in its path are imbed
or thrown aside. The ray's attraction is imbuing it with
terrific strength. It approaches the foreground of the
picture and we again cut back to:

The laboratory. Frankenstein, noting the time,
gives orders that all is over for the night. His first
assistant switches off the ray and the soul-shaking hum of
the giant generator ceases........

On the mountain side. The Monster. For an
instant the ray is still there; then it dies. Immediately,
freed from the compulsion of the ray, the Monster halts.
He rests ...... Now he can wander where he wills, and we
follow him while he strikes off down the slope towards the
fringes of a fir copse. As he walks we begin to hear, very
faintly, the shrill piteously squeaking cries of an animal
in pain. As the Monster advances the cries grow louder.
Suddenly they penetrate to such consciousness as he possesses.
He halts. He slowly turns his head in the direction of the
sound. The cries redouble and there comes from the Monster's
throat, as if in sympathy, a strangely similar sound. He
starts forward at a stumbling run......

Now a close-shot of a big hare. One of its hind
legs is caught in a steel trap. It is struggling to free
itself and giving vent to the pitiful sounds which we have
been hearing. There comes the sound of a crashing in the

undergrowth and the Monster's feet come into the picture.
The hare, terrified, redoubles its efforts. In another shot
we see the Monster. He drops to his knees beside the hare and
stares at it from out of his distorted face. It gives another cry. A similar sound, much softer, comes from the
Monster's throat and he sets huge blackened hands to the
jaws of the trap and wrenches it open. The hare dashes
off into the undergrowth and the Monster is left on his
knees staring after it. After a moment he is attracted
by something else - - this time by sight and not by sound.
We see that he has altered the angle of his head and, following the line of his vision, see a light shining through
the trees. He slowly rises and begins to move toward it.

In a close exterior shot we see the origin of
the light. It comes from the window of a little cottage.
The Monster comes into the edge of the picture, moving
steadily towards the light.

An interior of the cottage shows us the old
peasant who told the Sergeant the story of the mill. He
is seated at a table with his wife and two children - a
boy and a girl in their teens. They are happily playing
some primitive game of cards. They are intent upon the
game and so not see what we see - pressed against the glass
the horror which serves the Monster for a face. The face
is withdrawn. After a moment or two, during which the
small family, oblivious of any danger, continue their game,
the door is thrown open inwards with a crash. The old

man leaps to his feet. Bending his head to clear the lintel,
the Monster lurches into the room. His eyes are attracted
by the bright colours of the playing cards, and he makes
for the table. The woman screams. After a moment of
frozen horror the whole family dash for the farther door and
are gone. And now we see that the Monster is not actuated
by desire to harm humans. He will, as he does now, leave
them alone if they leave him alone. Such mind as he has is
on the bright colours of the cards and we see him sit in
the chair which the peasant has left and begin imitatively
to finger the cards......

But he tires. The colours cease to hold him.
The imitative process, like all imitative processes, loses
savour with repetition. He drops the cards. He pushes
back his chair, but does not rise. He hangs his bead and
rests his arms upon his thighs, the hands dangling down.
He stares with those terrible eyes into nothingness.....

And then (with an ultra quick dissolve) we come
to a close shot of Henry Frankenstein. He is, symbolically,
sitting in exactly the same position as this creation of
his which he still imagines to be a crumbling nothingness.
He, too, is staring into nothingness.......The Camera draws
away and we see that Frankenstein, who is now in ordinary
clothes, is seated in his drawing room. At the far side of
the room are members of the Delegation who have been at the
back of the laboratory while the experiment with the ray

was going on. The leader of the Delegation now crosses
the room and addresses Frankenstein. For a moment, lost in
his musing, Frankenstein does not hear. But at last he is
aroused and himself. He is told that the Delegation have
decided that if, after they have seen results of this even-
ing's experiment, they are satisfied that the ray does
everything that Frankenstein claims for it, they still want
one more test: but this time in connection with the special
clothing which Frankenstein and his assistant wear when they
may be exposed to the ray. Frankenstein laughs sardonically.
Questioned about the material, he abruptly refuses any in-
formation regarding it. Its texture and structure are as
much his secret as the ray itself. On the other hand he
acquiesces to the test, saying that such a test could take
place upon the following night- provided the Government
will agree - when he would be prepared to send his two
assistants out into the full force of the ray.

The Delegation then leaves and Frankenstein,
once more musing, is interrupted by his chief assistant,
Kurt. Kurt brings Frankenstein's coat and hat. Frankenstein stares at them, he is still lost in thought. Kurt
reminds him of the hospital and Frankenstein, with a start
sees that the time is nearly ten thirty. He hurries from
the house......

Now Elizabeth Frankenstein's room in the
hospital. Again Victor Moritz is with her. Elizabeth
has not improved. Victor is distraught about her. If not

for her own sake, then for that of others, she must will
herself to recover. Weakly she asks why. She is not
happy. She thinks that perhaps death would be pleasant.
Victor reminds her of her son. But he cannot resist men-
tioning himself as well. Weakly Elizabeth - her own mental
resistance lowered by her condition - holds out her hand
to him. It is plain tht at last, after all these years
she realizes that here is the man whom she really loves.
She is racked by a frssh spasm of pain. Victor wants
immediately to fetch her doctor but she stays him, and tells
him that she is oppressed, not only by her illness, but by
something else; something which she does not understand;
some queer sixth sense of impending ill. He attempts to
soothe her but does not succeed. She has even started
to refer to a similar feeling which she had once before
her marriage to Henry Frankenstein and when all the terror
of the Monster was at its height, when the doctor enters.
He is not pleased by her condition. He tells Victor that
he must go; the patient will be given an injection to make
her sleep. Victor, drawing the doctor aside, learns that
Elizabeth should be operated on. They are trying to avoid
it owing to her state, but now the doctor fears it will
be essential.....

Following Victor down the stairs we see him as
he is about to leave, meet Henry Frankenstein. No one may
see Elizabeth now, and the two men leave the hospital together.

    We go with them as they walk. Victor, his
heart wrung for Elizabeth, is enraged by Frankenstein,
and tells him, roundly, his opinion. Frankenstein defends
himself: he has been all day with the Delegation: they
are impressed. In a few days he will have solved the
world's problems: men will no longer be able to fight
and kill because there will always be other men banded
against them who have in their power such a destructive
weapon that not one will be able to face the threat of it.
Victor, however, is not impressed. He tells Frankenstein
that he should not dabble with death; should not forever
be trying to master secrets which are none of man's
business; should, instead, be human and think of human
things - - should not, in fact, try to usurp the power of
the gods. The argument develops, each man bitterly de-
fending his own point of view. They come to the parting
of their ways. They halt, but the discussion is not
finished. Enraged by what he considers his friend's
stubborness, Victor finally refers to Frankenstein's first
disastrous experiment. He recalls the horror of the
Monster. But he is cut short by Henry Frankenstein who
angrily tells him not to delve about the past! "All that,"
says Frankenstein, "is dead! Dead and buried!" He swings
on his heal and walks away and as he goes we fade out......

    We fade in to a small clearing in a fir wood
on the lower slope of the mountainside. It is sunset on
the following day. A ring of mountaineers - perhaps

thirty of forty men - are surrounding something upon the
ground. They are all stern-faced. At one side of the
picture are lying three disabled men, their hurts being
attended to by a comrade. Suddenly there is a violent
movement in the center of the ring of men and from their
midst comes a dreadful cry which we recognize: the half-
animal cry of the Monster in pain.

The groups shifts and the camera angle changes
and we see that in the center of the ring of men, lying
upon the ground, is the writhing figure of the Monster...
He has been overpowered by sheer numbers and is now bound
with strong ropes. His arms are lashed behind him and to
them have been lashed his feet, drawn torturingly back.
His cry dies away but a second later we see what has
caused it. One of the foremost men in the group steps
forward and kicks at the unprotected head. The nailed
boot thuds against the Monster's skull and once more we
hear the cry and see the bound creature writhing in effort to free itself......

Now the older heads among the captors draw
aside in counsel. They have caught the Thing! What shall
they do? Two are for immediately dragging the captive
back to the village and letting responsibility rest upon
the shoulders of the Authority! Two are against this and say
that it should be put to death here and now. But then
yet another shows them the impossibility of this course.

How can they destroy this - it is not a man!
Consider: this was the Thing that went down under the

burning mill years before. It is a fiend from Hell!
And then there joins the group the poor crazed Otto-
the peasant whose little daughter years before was killed
by the Thing. His eyes are blazing; and an impassioned
speech burst from him. The others are forced to listen
and as they listen, they realize that out of this dis-
ordered mind has come the solution. Otto is talking of the
light that comes across the mountains which brings
death to it: the light which came last night when they
had to keep their cattle in and not go near the path of
the light; the light that the Burgomaster has told them
is to come again tonight! They have seen what the light
does. Has it not killed and blackened every blade of
grass, every shrub, every tree? Has it not even killed
the goats that have strayed? Nothing, nothing, can live
within it........

There is a swelling chorus of agreement and
once more all the men surge round the prostrate Monster.

We dissolve to the same group in a different
setting and at night. As the group shifts and the camera
pulls back we see that they are now at one edge of the
path that the ray has carved - the path that lies straight
across the country like a black scar. The Monster, still
in his torturing bonds, is thrust, by the staves of the
mountaineers, into the very center of the path. A member
of the band shouts hoarsely that soon the light will be
coming. They take to their heels. Only one man is left
looking at the Monster - the crazed Otto. He leans over

37

the Monster and spits down upon him. He turns and runs
after his fellows into the gathering darkness and safety....

The is a moment during which we dimly see the
figure of the Monster struggling against its bonds. And
then, with a terrible suddenness, comes the grey light of
the ray. The Monster is right in its path. As it strikes
him and pains him with its power of its attraction for the
Monster. He jerks convulsively. Despite his bonds he gets
to his knees; he begins to scramble along upon them, falling every now and then upon his face .... And then the
brightness of the ray increases and we know that miles
away, in the laboratory, Frankenstein has increased its
power. A harsh cry comes from the Monster's throat. He
is on his knees. He falls. Another cry breaks from him
and with a terrific and convulsive effort he snaps one of
the ropes which bind him. We see him close. We see the
ropes part one after the other.... And then we see him,
on his feet again, blindly stumbling - one arm again across
his face - up along the path of the ray ....

We are back in the laboratory again. Frankenstein is alone, at the control board.

We are in a small ante room to the laboratory,
Members of the Delegation are there. They are looking out,
through a great telescope, along the path of the ray. We
see through the telescope. Far away, just entering a
crevice in the foothills, are two curious figures. We
realize from what we see and from scraps of dialogue that

these are Frankenstein's two assistants. This is the
test of the textalite protection against the ray. The
two small figures are right in the center of the path of
the ray and they are plodding on unharmed. They disappear
into the foothills.

We go back to Frankenstein in the laboratory.
He is working at the control dials. The buzzer of a
telephone sounds through the biant hum of the generator.
He sets his dials and goes to a wall telephone and speaks.
The leader of the Delegation is speaking to him from the
next room. He is saying that the Delegation is satisfied;
that the test, so far as they are concerned, can stop now.
Frankenstein answers: "I told them to go so far; they
shall go. It will take fifteen minutes yet. During those
fifteen minutes the ray is going to be at full strength!"
He hangs up the telephone and goes back to his controls
and we see the needle of the dial of the power gauge jerk
over to a thousand full strength ! ......

In the foothills between the town and the
mountainside. Across the darkness the ray is streaming.
Up a slope in the background of the picture toil the
queer figures in texalite and masks. We follow them,
coming closer to them. They top a small rise and start
to descend. Now they are in the foreground of the picture
and the camera is just behind them. Suddenly, over their
heads, we see coming along the ray towards them the jerk-
ing shambling dreadful figure of the Monster. Between
them and it a large tree - killed the night before - is
lying across the path. Its multitudinous branches stick
upwards so that we see the figure of the Monster through
a sort of dead tracery. The two masked figures plod onwards - they have not seen him.

Now we see the two masked figures approaching
the tree from one side and the Monster arriving at the
far side. Imprlled by the attraction of the ray he must
go on. He tries to climb but the awkward branches
prevent him. He starts savagely to clear a path. Flail-
ing with his arms he breaks the branches, snapping them
off like so many twigs...

The two masked figures have seen him. They
stop aghast. We see him from their viewpoint, a
monstrous, incredible figure smashing and ploughing in-
credibly towards them. Petrification past, they turn
to run. One figure - it is Kurt - dashes out of the ray,
to one side. The other runs blindly, straight onward,
back along the way he has come. But he has not gone more
than a few paces before he catches his foot and falls

heavily. The shock dislodges the visor of his helmet
and we see the face of the second assistant. He twitches
once, seems to shrink and lies still - the ray has sucked
out his life. Into the picture - taken up almost wholly
by the dead body - plough the feet of the Monster. They
stride over him and are gone....

The laboratory again. Frankenstein, after a
glance at his watch, turns off the switch of the generator.
The ray dies. The hum of the generator ceases. He takes
off his mask and stripping the gloves from his hands,
walks toward the laboratory door, unbolts it and crosses
to the ante-room. He is greeted by the Delegation; they
are enthusiastic. Frankenstein listens to them. The
leader tells him definitely that his offer will be ac-
cepted. He smiles wearily. They begin to ask him
questions. They say they want to know how long it will
take for them to establish a station. He says two or
three months. They are horror stricken: this is too long.
And then Frankenstein astounds them. He says, in effect,
that there is no need for them to establish a generator
and a station. They can work from here. The effective
radius of the ray is at least one thousand miles, and
all they need, in the present crises, is a six hundred
mile range at most. Questions rain upon him again. How
can he focus the ray? He silences the questioners. He
says: "Come with me!" and walks back into the laboratory.
On the threshold the leader of the Delegation halts;
they have seen the effect of the ray. They are afraid
to enter. Frankenstein - and here he shows definitely
the terrific strain under which he is - laughs at them

with a mad uproariousness in his laughter. They enter,
sheep-like. He says: "Do not be afraid, gentlemen!...
Now watch!" Beside the shaft upon which the huge glittering box of the Projector stands is a large steel lever.
Frankenstein pulls this back. "Watch!" he says again, and
slowly, inexorable, the shaft begins smoothly to rise,
carrying the Projector with it.

The visitor gape upwards. Frankenstein crosses
to the control board and pushes a switch. With a rumbling sound the whole of one half of the laboratory roof
slides back. Slowly the great shaft mounts, carrying the
Projector. Up it goes and up. The Projector reaches the
roof, passes beyond it....

Frankenstein moves back the lever. The shaft
ceases to rise. Frankenstein goes back to the control
board and glances at a gauge. He says: "We are upon a
hill. The Projector is now one hundred feet above the
highest point of that hill. It is not at the full of its
height - but from where it is a single man could wipe
out anyone of twenty European cities!" ....

Now we see the Delegation leaving. It is ar-
ranged that they shall meet at noon upon th enext day
for the final arrangements. Alone, Frankenstein goes
back to his laboratory. He makes at once for the lever
which controls the power by which the shaft in raised and
lowered, but he has not touched the Lever when he is interrupted. There comes a sound of running, staggering
footsteps and Kurt's voice, shouting hoarsely. Frankenstein stares; then hastens toward the door. He reaches

the door at the moment that Kurt enters. At the sight of
his employer Kurt's strength fails him and he collapses.
Frankenstein, concerned, tends him. When the man has recovered his strength he begins to gasp out his story, and,
as he begins, we cut away to:

The Monster. The ray is gone, he is free again.
It is very dark and we can only see him dimly. We do not
know where he is, but after a moment we see that he comes
to a low wall of stone. He climbs this and is lost to
view....

Back in the laboratory. Kurt has plainly come
to the end of his story, and it is clear that Frankenstein
has gathered its full and terrifying import. The Monster
is resuscitated. Kurt is saying: "It can't be! It's
impossible! Impossible!" But Frankenstein, all colour
drained from his face, shakes his head. He says: "It is
only too possible! I was mad not to see the possibility.
Mad!" Kurt insists that this thing could not have happened; that what he saw could not be the creature of
Frankenstein's cration. But Frankenstein silences him;
and briefly, in a dead monotone, makes clear what has
happened. The Thing he created was given life elec-
trically; its life-force was not the life-force of man
as we know men. Therefore the death of man, as we know
death, could not ever overtake him. And now the very
man who created this Thing - himself - has created another
force! And this other force is so utterly the negation
of the force with which he have life to the Thing, that
so far from destroying that life it revivifies it and

draws it toward itself. A positive must be drawn toward
a more powerful negative. "But then," says Kurt, horror-
stricken, "this... this Thing can never be destroyed!"
"It can!" says Frankenstein. "And it must be! It must be
destroyed by the very thing that has brought it back!"
He suddenly jerks himself out of this musing upon his
horror. The Monster must be found and caught. He gives
rapid orders to Kurt to collect all the manservants. But,
at this stage, no word must be given to the Authorities.
He himself telephones to Victor and we leave him at the
telephone and cut to:

The exterior of Frankenstein's house. The
search party, collected, is setting out upon its mission.
We see them, their way lighted by flashlights and torches,
march out through the gardens of the house and on to the
plain across which the scar of the ray lies black. As the
lights of the little procession dwindle, we slowly dissolve.....

The next morning, in the garden of Frankenstein's house. Down a flight of steps from the first
terrace come Franstein's son and his nurse. The nurse
carries under her arm a big gaily-striped ball. The child
is laughing. The nurse sets him down at the edge of the
lawn. She begins to roll the ball towards him. Delighted,
the child rolls the ball back, giving small fat chuckles
of delight. The nurse, talking to the child all the time
begins gradually to increase the distance over which they
are rolling the ball and, at last, being near the corner
of a shrubbery, picks up the ball and disappears round

the corner. The child stares; then opens its mouth to
cry and then chuckles as the ball comes rolling out towards him from behind the shrubs. From a close shot of
the child receiving the ball with delight and gleefully
pushing it back again swe cut to a shot of the nurse in
hiding. Behind her is a large tree, and even as she
stoops to stop the ball which rolls into the picture, we
see the Monster slowly draw out from behind the tree-trunk.
The nurse rolls the ball back and again we cut to a close
shot of the child. He is reaching out for the ball.

"Now the nurse again. The Monster is standing
immediately behind her. He is obviously watching, fascinated, the progress of the brightly coloured sphere. A
little noise comes from his throat. The nurse turns
sharply. Her eyes widen in terror. Her mouth opens...
but she is too much in the grip of terror to speak. She
makes a violent movement as if to get to her feet. The
Monster glances down at her. Her sudden movement has
made him feel that he is about to be attacked. He strikes
at her and she falls over limply. Immediately his eyes
leave her prone body and avidly watch the approaching
ball. It rolls into the picture. The Monster drops
awkwardly to his knees, picks up the ball, twists it
this way and that in his hand and looks at it. He puts
it down and, imitating grotesquely the nurse's action,
rolls it back again.

From a close shot of the child receiving the
ball we cut to the exterior of the garden. The search
party, headed by Henry Frankenstein and Victor, is re-

turning; worn and dejected. They are about to turn in at
a gate in the low stone wall when suddenly Victor who is
looking into the garden, stops and clutches at Frankenstein's arm. He points, and in a shot taken from his and
Henry Frankenstein's viewpoint, we see the child sitting
happily upon the brass while there emerges from behind a
shrub the frightful figure of the still kneeling Monster.
He has the ball in his arms and is working his way forward
upon his knees. The child looks toward him. It is
puzzled, but is too young to be afraid.

After a moment's horror-stricken immobility,
Frankenstein and Victor and other members of the search
party vault the wall and rush towards the child. The
father snatches up the child. The Monster gives one look
at the number of men who are rushing at him, rises to his
feet, drops the ball, turns and flies, and is lost to view
among the trees and shrubs. As he goes there comes floating back to their ears, a snarling cry of anger.....

We now see varying shots of the pursuit. Henry
Frankenstein has stayed momentarily behind to place his
child in safe keeping and the search is now headed by
Victor.

We see the Monster fleeing ungainly down narrow
side streets, running wildly and with no sense of direction. Every now and then the fearful sight of him strikes
a passerby with terror. Always, however, he is one turn
ahead of his pursuers and it is only by reason of the
directions of the persons who have seen him that his
pursuers manage to keep upon his trail. We see him again,
following a shot of the pursuers. He is in a high alley-

way between two brick walls. In the right-hand brick wall
there is a door standing ajar. He sees it, pushes it open
and enters. The door swings to behind him....

Now the operating theatre of the hospital.
Elizabeth Frankenstein is on the table. The surgeon is
standing beside the table. The anesthetist is pronouncing
her ready. A nurse is standing behind. The surgeon turns
to the trolley upon which are his instruments and as the
camera moves to show him selecting one knife from a
glittering case of them, we see the door behind him opening slowly. The movement is soundless and it is only
casually that the nurse glances towards the door. But we
see her face and we know what the fully opened door has
reavealed. A strangled cry comes from her and she drops in
a dead faint. The anaethetist, now looking over his
shoulder, rushes toward her but the surgeon has seen
what the nurse saw. He turns slowly, his eyes wide. The
camera moves and we see the Monster slowly advancing.
His eyes are fastened upon the white operating table
and the figure upon it. He is beset by dim memories of
a time when he was on a table like that and a man clad
like this man in a long white garment was bending over
him with one of those glittering things in his hand....

The doctor bars his path. The Monster puts
out a mighty hand and with another of his flail-like
blows, fells the interferer. The anaethetist turns and
leaps up. He is horrified but he puts himself between
the advancing Monster and the operating table. But his

courage is useless. The giant hands meet about his
neck. Their grip tightens and he too sinks to the floor.
The Monster draws near and nearer. His gaze is caught by
the glitter of the knives. He stops. He looks down at
them. Struggling memories flicker their shadow across
his face. He picks up one of the knives clumsily. He
goes nearer to the table. He bends over it. He looks at
the thing upon the table and then at the shining thing
in his hand. He bends over the table -

And Victor Moritz dashes into the theatre
followed by men of the search party. The Monster looks
at them. He snarls with rage. His lips draw back. For
a moment it seems as if he will do battle and then more
men come into the room. He knows now that numbers can be
too much for him. He throws down the knife and leaps
across the room in ungainly strides and vanishes through
a far door. Victor, waving the men on in pursuit, bends
with ghastly face over the operating table. Other members
of the search party rush out of the far door in pursuit
of the Monster. Henry Frankenstein comes in. He is
breathless. He rushes to the table and stands beside
Victor. The shape upon the table stares. Elizabeth is
coming out of the anaesthetic. She is still unconscious,
but a word bursts from her lips. It is a man's name,
but it is not her husband's. "Victor" she says. Frankenstein stares. He turns slowly to look at his friend.
But then before either of them can speak, a sound comes
to their ears - and ours.

It is the faint far off hum of the giant generator. It is unmistakable. Frankenstein clasps his

head with his hands. A horrified sound comes from him
and he turns and runs madly from the room.

The laboratory. At first glance it seems
empty - but the hum of the generator fills the air. As
the camera moves about the huge chamber we suddenly see
the Monster. He is at the control board. The camera
swiftly comes up to a close shot and we see that he is
playing - in the intense absorbtion of a child - with all
the glittering switches and wheels upon the board. From
this shot of him, intent upon these bright things that
twist and turn, we suddenly go, with a quick dissolve to:

A scene which we have not viewed before. It is
a broad main street in a modern city. It is a busy hour
in the day. The sidewalks are thronged with people and
the raod with traffic...and then, invisible because of
the daylight, the ray strikes.... Chaos....Vehicles, their
drivers and passengers instantaneously killed, go on with
their own momentum and crash into walls and into each
other.... Pedestrains fall, with a slow, wilting....
Giant sparks shoot from the cables of trolley cars. Trees
at the edge of the sidewalks crumple and fall as the men
and women beneath them have crumpled and fallen...... Within an instant, this scene of busy vivid life becomes of
still and utter death.....

Faintly across a grey sky we see a big passen-
ger plane winging its way. Suddenly it comes into the
lane of unseen death. Its smooth flight is interrupted.
It rolls from side to side, plunges quickly, and then
drops earthward like a plumment......

The laboratory again. Still the Monster is
absorbed. Now he has found the wheel which controls the
direction of the ray. He is swinging this backwards and
forwards. He likes the glitter of the light upon its
spokes.....

Outside the laboratory. Frankenstein and Victor,
with the rest of the party hard at their heels, rush up
to the door. But at the door Frankenstein halts. He turns
to the men behind him. They wish to rush in in a body
and overpower the Monster. But Frankenstein says "no".
He explains in short staccato sentences. The Monster
must be drawn from the control board. A struggle at the
board may means seconds, which will blot out thousands of
lives. He, himself must go in alone. He is the one being for whom the Monster has feelings, and that feeling
is hatred. His presence, alone, will lead the Monster
to him. When he shouts, then they can enter. He goes in,
slamming the door behind him.

Inside the laboratory. The Monster wheels at
the noise of the steel door. Frankenstein walks toward
him. The Monster glares. He has remembered. This is
the man whom he hates. He leaves the control board. He
shuffles towards Frankenstein, and then he rushes. His
great arms go about Frankenstein as Frankenstein shouts...

The door opens and men rush in. Victor rushes
to the switch and turns it off and the humming of the
generator ceases. A little mob of men hurl themselves
on the Monster. We slowly dissolve to:

The laboratory still; but now there are only
three men in it. Three men - and the Thing which is not

a man. The Thing is seated. It is upon a steel chair,
the legs of which are clamped to the floor. It immediately
faces the Projector, which is now lowered to the position
in which we first saw it. The Thing is motionless - because it cannot be otherwise. Not ropes but steel bands
and chains bind its arms and legs to the arm and legs
of the chair, and more chains are about the body. Only
its head can move, and that very slightly. Behind it
stand the three men. They are Henry Frankenstein, Victor
Moritz and Kurt. Frankenstein is pale and there is an
ugly wound upon his forehead. But he is composed. His
voice is more tranquil than we have heard it and his
whole manner altered. Victor is saying: "But what are
you going to do?" Frankenstein says: 'I am going to
put and end to It.' And by It we know that he means the
Thing of his creation. He explains more fully than he
has to Kurt that the life he himself put into this Thing
can be drawn out by the death which is also the child of
his brain. He asks Victor and Kurt to go. They are unwilling to leave him, Victor is especial sensing something
which he cannot understand. He assures them that he will
be "all right - quite all right" - - and bids them return
in fifteen minutes. They go.....

Carefully Frankenstein closes the great steel
door behind them and then, slowly, he walks over to the
center of the chamber and stands looking down over to the
center of the chamber and stands looking down at the helpless Thing. Its eyes glare at him, and, once, a strangled
cry comes from its constricted throat. In Frankenstein's
face, now, as he looks, there is for the first time no

horror. There is only in his eyes a great compassion....

He puts a hand to his head and walks away. We
see him now seated at a table in a far corner. He is
writing furiously....He ceases. He puts something in an
envelope, seals the envelope and addresses it. He picks
up the envelope and with it another piece of paper and
walks out of picture...

The camera, moving, does not follow Frankenstein.
It centers upon the chair and the occupant of the chair.
After a moment Frankenstein comes back. Once more he
stands by the chair. Once more he looks down. And then,
suddenly, he moves. He puts a hand upon the shoulder of
the helpless Thing. And he says: 'I am sorry. Sorry.'

For a moment created and creator look into
each others eyes and for a moment we see in the eyes of
the Thing a sudden softening....

Frankenstein turns away. He goes to the control
board. He twists the direction-wheel until the Projector
is facing directly at the Monster.

He presses the generator switch. Once again
the giant humming fills the air. The ray shoots out.
We can see it in the dim light. It strikes the Monster
and for a moment we watch in horror while he tries to
burst his bonds, drawn by the irresistible force of the
negation of his own life-spark. But this time the bonds
hold. A frightful convulsion passes over the figure and
then there seems to rush out of it a vivid, blinding
flash....

The Thing does not move. By reason of its
bonds the body cannot even sag, but we know that it is

dead. Frankenstein comes into the picture. He is not in
the ray but just at its edge. He is not clothed in textalite. He looks down at the dead Thing. He says again:
"I am sorry." And he says too; "My fault. All my fault".
And then he takes a step forward, towards the ray.

And immediately we come to the anteroom. The
hum still fills the air. Victor is pacing up and down.
He is anxious. At last he crosses the room and opens
the door and walks across to the steel door to the laboratory. His eye is caught by a piece of paper and an envelope which protrude from beneath the door. He looks
again and then stoops and picks them up. Upon one is
written: "Send Kurt in, in textalite, turn off switch."
And upon the envelope, Victor reads his own name......

THE END

(Note: This is the real end. But a tag
would probably be needed. If so
nothing could be easier. A Fade-
and then Victor and a convalescent
Elizabeth. And Frankenstein's son.
And a reference to Frankenstein and
now, by bequeathing the Ray, he did
in the end, after all benefit humanity....)

Outline Treatment For

File No. 6265

Picture No. _____

Only Copy

"THE RETURN OF FRANKENSTEIN"

Blockman

Against a weirdly lighted background of
grotesquely jagged mountains, a crowd of a dozen peasants
are attacking the Frankenstein monster with clubs and
swords. The monster is at bay under a tree of bizarre
shape. He is beating his attacker off with a huge branch
snatched from the tree. A little apart from the crowd
we see the figures of Henry Frankenstein and Elizabeth.
Henry has an axe in his hand as he embraces his wife.

"Why must you risk your life like this?"
Elizabeth is saying in a voice that seems to belong to
someone else. "There are enough without you."

"I created this monster with my own hands,"
Henry replies, "and with my own hands I must destroy him."

Henry skirts the crowd and chops down the
tree with a few swift strokes. The peasants scatter but
the monster is caught beneath the falling tree.

We hear laughter and hand clapping. The
camera pulls back rapidly, revealing that the scene which
appeared to be a long shot was actually a close shot of a
puppet show. As the camera pulls further back and pans,
we see the applauding audience seated on wooden benches.
Flapping canvas, acetylene flares, and other detail and
wagon wheels beneath the stage of the puppet show tell
us we are with a travelling carnival.

The camera next looks down through the top
of the puppet theater through the maze of threads that control the marionettes. We see the puppeteers' hands --

one pair delicate and feminine, the other unmistakably masculine.

The camera pans upward to disclose that the
hands belong to Henry Frankenstein and Elizabeth. They smile
happily and as the applause continues off scene Elizabeth
places her cheek against Henry's in a gesture of contented
affection.

Outside, at a far corner of the carnival,
a barker is attracting crowds in front of a tent which,
according to the gaudy canvas banner, shelters Fifi, the
giantess, and Meta and Greta, the Siamese twins. A stranger
in a long black cloak, the collar of which muffles his face,
asks the barker if Henry Frankenstein is with the show.
The barker shakes his head in the negative.

The cloaked traveller, whose distinguished
bearing contrasts with that of the peasant patrons of the
carnival, walks on through the street fair. We hear a
background of characteristic carnival noises: a steam
caliope playing 'The Blue Danube Waltz' somewhere in the
distance while a tzigane violinist fiddles soulfully, if
discordantly, and hoarsed-voiced spielers harangue the
murmuring crowds. The cloaked stranger continues to ask
unsuccessfully for Frankenstein. He passes ~~Emil~~ Emma, the lion
tamer, who is strutting in front of ~~his~~ her cages for the
edification of open-mouthed yokels; Arnaldo, the magician,
whose big act consists of sawing in half his blonde assistant, Sari, in pink silk tights; Hans, the small bespectacled caliope player who looks particularly tiny at the
keyboard of his steam piano. None of them knows Frankenstein.
The stranger pauses in front of a garish flare-lighted banner announcing the Heinrich marionettes. He studies the

crude puppet characters painted on the canvas and a hopeful expression crosses his face as he sees the effigy of
the monster. He buys a ticket and goes in.

Inside the tent the puppets are performing
a Harlequin-Columbine playlet. In the accompanying dialogue the stranger apparently recognizes the voices of
Henry and Elizabeth. When the ~~tiny~~ *diminutive* curtain falls, he
rushes from the tent and around to the back of the caravan, which serves both as stage and living quarters for
the puppeteers. He knocks on the door calling: "Henry,
Henry Frankenstein!"

Inside the caravan Henry and Elizabeth are
hooking the threads of their marionettes into the tiny
cleats in the top of the stage. They look at each other
in alarm. The stranger continues to knock and call Henry's
name.

"There's no one here by that name," says
Henry without opening the door.

"It's Paul," the stranger insists. "Open
up, Henry."

Henry throws open the door and there is a
joyous reunion.

"Paul, how did you ever find us?"

"You don't think I'd let my best friend disappear out of my life without making every effort to trace
him?" Paul replies.

From the ensuing dialogue we discover that
the monster that Frankenstein created reappeared after
his supposed death in the burning mill. The monster's continued terrorization of the countryside brought death to
Baron Frankenstein, ruin to the Frankenstein fortune, and
the enmity of the villagers to Henry and his bride.

-4-

"I hope you didn't think," says Henry, "that my flight was the result of cowardice. I'm not the sort of man to let a pack of ~~embittered~~ villagers drive me from my ~~ancestral~~ home."

"I understand," says Paul. " It was on account of Elizabeth."

"Elizabeth was quite ready to stand by me," says Henry, "at home or anywhere. But If I had stayed at home, I would have had to dip my hands again in human blood."

"Blood!"

"The monster's outbursts of murder and destruction can be partly explained by the fact that he was alone in a hostile world that was repulsed by his hideousness. He made it clear that he expected me to change this."

A horrified expression creeps into Paul's face as he realizes the import of Henry's words.

"My God, Henry!" he exclaims. "You wouldn't inflict another horrible creature on the world?"

"Of course not," says Henry, ~~smiling~~. "It was to avoid being forced to create a mate for the monster that ~~Elizabeth and~~ I have lost ~~our~~ my identity -- and found happiness -- with this travelling carnival. Our name, by the way, is now Heinrich."

Henry is called to give a short encore. As the curtain rises on the puppet show again, we cut to a shot of the monster lifting the canvas to crawl into the tent. There is a sinister threat in his slow, clumsy movements as he looks about with mad, haunted eyes and sits down on the end of a bench occupied by some children who are too interested in the performance to notice the uncouth giant next to them. We watch the performance over the massive hunched

Frankessler bows again, and when we again
cut to the monster, we see an empty stair—
-5-   the monster

shoulders of the monster for an instance. There is a burst
of applause and we see Henry step into the tiny stage like
a giant in proportion to his marionettes. He has to stoop
in order to be seen within the miniature proscenium as he
takes his bows. We cut back to the applauding audience and
see that the monster has disappeared from the bench beside
the children.

The performance over, Henry rejoins Paul
and Elizabeth. He opens a bottle of wine to celebrate the
reunion.

"Frankenstein 1885," says Henry. "I managed
to salvage two bottles when we left home. I've been saving
them for an occasion like this."

Cutting outside, we show a giant specter-like
shadow moving across canvassed tent walls and distorted by the
uneven sides of carnival wagons. We hear the confusion of
fair ground noises which carry over as we return to Henry,
Paul, and Elizabeth drinking a toast. They look up startled,
their glasses poised in mid-air, as wild discordant shrieks
issue from the pipes of the steam caliope. Savage roars
echo from the cages of the wild animals.

We see the monster seated at the caliope pound-
ing the keyboard madly with his great hands. He laughs
crazily as he hits on the same note, making it hoot with
ominous insistence. We see flashes of Henry and Paul leaving the caravan in alarm. We see a frightened reaction from
the crowd milling about the sideshows. Rudolph, the carnival
proprietor, starts running toward the caliope. Hans, the
bespectacled caliope player, interrupts a musical discussion
with Lothar, the violinist, to join in the chase. The wild
hoot of the caliope which has been continuing over these
scenes ceases abruptly with a terrific discord.

58

When the startled men arrive at the caliope,
the monster has vanished. Hans is puzzled. Paul and Henry
look at each other with apprehension, but Rudolph merely says:
"Those damned kids," as we FADE OUT.

We FADE IN on a long shot of the train of
carnival wagons silhouetted against a moonlit horizon. As
the caravan winds its way over the hill toward Bratislava, *many miles*
~~several weeks~~ distant, the monster watches it pass. He is
crouched behind a boulder, his inhuman face ghastly in the
moonlight. In a series of closer shots we pick up the wagons
one by one. We see Rudolph, the horse-faced proprietor, discussing his future plans -- whether he should disband his
show on reaching Bratislava, or reorganize it to tour the
warmer latitudes of southern Italy during the winter. The
swinging beams from a lantern suspended from one of the
shafts throws strange shadows on his gaunt features.

We see Arnaldo, the magician, a thin, dark,
taciturn man with black, beady, sinister eyes and sensitive
fingers. His high, broad cheek bones give a triangular ap-
pearance to his face with his thin-lipped mouth and sharp chin
at the apex. He rides with Sari, his assistant. We learn
that this shapely blonde with a hard exotic beauty is madly
in love with Arnaldo and expects to bear his child in Bratislava late in the winter.

We see Hans, the caliope player who doubles
on the cymbalon, riding atop his steam piano with Lothar,
the tzigane violinist. Hans, who is plump, blonde, with a
high receding forehead and thick glasses, shows Lothar a
photograph of his fiancee who is meeting him in Bratislava
to get married. The gentle soulful-eyed Lothar who wears
his hair long in a Kubelik bob has lent his favorite violin
to a friend -- "This outdoor travelling is not good for fine
violins and my friend plays indoor engagements in summer

Kursaals" -- and Lothar knows from experience that if he
arrives in Bratislava too late in the fall the friend will
have pawned the instrument to buy an overcoat.

We see Emma, the lion tamer, a masculine
looking woman with the shadow of a mustache on her upper
lip, putting her arm affectionately around Fifi, the giantess.
In the same tone she uses to address her lions she boasts
of how she beats her husband into submission whenever she
sees him in Bratislava. Her tone is more tender as she
tells Fifi of her general contempt for all men.

The monster is crashing through the under-
brush in pursuit of the carnival wagons. Branches snap and
saplings fall as he plunges ponderously forward, his arms
swinging like flails. Breaking through to a clear view of
the road, he pauses to breath in prolonged sibillant blasts
which make plumes of vapor on the frosty night air. On the
roar beyond the carnival wagons are passing. The camera
trolleys forward, picks up Henry's wagon, and stays with
it as we listen to dialogue.

Henry, Elizabeth, and Paul are riding on
the driver's seat. Paul and Elizabeth are doing most of
the talking. Henry appears to be darkly preoccupied and
answers only in monosyllables.

"Henry can hardly wait until we get to
Bratislava," Elizabeth is saying, "because Herr Doktor
Zauber lives there now! Remember him? He used to be
one of Henry's professors at Ingloatadt University."

"So he does hanker for his old scientific
life," says Paul.

"Not at all," Henry grunts.

"He does," says Elizabeth. "I am sure he
will be puttering around in Professor Zauber's laboratory
all winter."

"I never want to see another test tube,"
says Henry gruffly.

Elizabeth and Paul comment on Henry's sullen mood.

"I have been vaguely uneasy ever since last night," Henry explains. "I can't help wondering if the monster couldn't have followed you here, Paul."

"Not likely," says Paul.

"Stop worrying," says Elizabeth.

Henry laughs at his own fears. He pulls the horses to a stop and insists that Elizabeth and Paul get some sleep in order that one of them may take the reins toward morning.

The moon hangs low over the hills as Henry, alone on the driver's seat, starts his horses again. He has dropped a little behind the other carnival wagons. Inside the caravan Elizabeth and Paul are rolled in blankets asleep. A claw-like hand parts the thicket beside the road. The monster lunges forward through the opening and follows the caravan with long, ungainly steps.

Henry is drowsing. His chin falls sleepily on his chest. The reins are slack in his inert hands. Left to themselves, the horses have slowed their pace and the last of the other carnival wagons disappears around a turn far down the road. The monster runs alongside Henry's wagon with a queer, crouching, animal-like gait. He looks up at Henry who is now sound asleep. His fingers are like talons as he darts his long arm toward one of the horses.

The camera angle is now on the sleeping Henry, shooting from above toward the rear of the moving wagon. The body of a black horse is lying in the road behind. A following shot from the rear shows us the wagon leaving the road, bumping and careening down a gentle slope. In the foreground is the body of a white horse. The sleeping Henry stirs uneasily on the driver's seat. The wheels crunch through

stubble and lift gratingly over rocks. Henry awakens, pulls
instinctively at the reins, then drops them. His eyes widen
with horror. His wagon is no longer being drawn by horses.
In the traces the giant, mishapen form of the monster looms,
his huge hands grasping the shafts, plodding forward with strides as
slow inexorable strides like the march of fate.

Suppressing an exclamation, Henry applies the
brakes. The monster turns in the traces. He grimaces hide-
ously over his shoulder. He snarls between his fang-like
teeth.

Henry leaps down from the wagon. The monster
drops the shafts and springs at him. There is a brief, furious struggle. Henry is no match for the inhuman strength of
the monster who pinions his hands, throws him across his
shoulders like a bag of meal and starts off into the woods.
Elizabeth and Paul are still asleep inside the caravan.

Henry's first impulse is to call for help, but
realizing that Paul and Elizabeth could do nothing more than
expose themselves to danger, he remains silent. As the monster continues to plunge deeper into the woods, Henry addresses him. His desperate monologue is like the speech
of a man talking to himself, for Henry knows that his creation
lacks the power of replying.

"Where are you taking me?" Henry demands.
"You won't kill me. You know you can't kill me. Let me
down!"

Guttural growls are the monster's only an-
swer. He emerges from the woods into a stony ravine through
which a mountain torrent is rushing. He dumps Henry on the
rocky bank almost at the brink of a roaring waterfall which
is churning a smother of dead-white foam fifty feet below

in the waning light of the moon.

"I know what you want," says Henry, "You expect to frighten me into making you a mate. I won't do it."

The monster stands over Henry in a menacing posture but makes no sound or movement. Only the roar of the waterfall breaks the stillness.

"I refuse to create another monster like you," Henry continues. "I refuse now as I refused before. You can't force me to do it. You can threaten me, but you can't kill me. I'm the only man in the world who can give you what you want. If you kill me, you destroy all hope for yourself."

Henry laughs, almost hysterically. He gets to his feet. The monster's ominous silence continues.

"~~You can't bully a Frankenstein!~~" Henry shouts. "I'll never consent to another fiendish creation and you can't force me. Never!"

Henry starts to go. The monster pounces upon him, snarling. Dragging Henry after him, the monster wades into the stream. He braces himself at the brink of the waterfall, grasps Henry in his great arms, and holds him so that his head protrudes beyond the edge. Again Henry's eyes widen.

In the boiling, swirling pool at the foot of the falls, Henry reads the monster's message. There, caught between two black rocks, is the dead face of a young girl. The pallid, wet features of the corpse, Henry realizes, might have been those of Elizabeth.

The monster has touched Henry in his most vulnerable spot. The wordless threat has changed his defiance to supplication.

"Don't touch Elizabeth," he pleads. "Promise that you won't harm Elizabeth and I -- I'll make you a mate."

Queer sounds like the purring of a cat issue from the monster's lips which are contorted into a grimace

that was meant to be a smile. A gleam of Henry's old defiance
again comes to the surface.

"But you'll do your part!" he exclaims. "You'll
do your share of this grisly business! You'll steal the ~~female~~
bodies that I am to imbue with unnatural life."

The monster continues to purr. Henry turns and *flees*
~~runs~~ into the woods. The monster does not move.

We dissolve to a shot of Henry awakening a
farmer with whom he bargains for the purchase of two horses.
After another dissolve, we see Henry's wagon drawn along the
road by the new horses. Dawn is breaking. Inside the caravan
Elizabeth and Paul are still asleep. Henry's face is grim.
He raps on the side of the wagon calling. "Paul! Paul!".

When Paul's head appears, Henry says. "I want
you to go to Bratislava immediately. Get there the quickest
way possible and see Professor Zauber. He'll land you some
instruments that you will bring back to me in the next town."

Paul is aghast. "But Henry," he exclaims,
"Surely you're not thinking of --"

"The monster has found me," says Henry.

"But Henry --" protests Paul again.

"I'm not going to sacrifice Elizabeth. That's
definite. Will you go to Bratislava for me?"

Reluctantly Paul agrees.

Henry's caravan comes upon the other carnival
wagons encamped outside the walls of a medieval-looking village.
Smoke is arising on the early morning air from the crooked
stove pipes of the wagons. Preparations for breakfast are
going on. Rudolph greets Henry with a steaming mug of coffee
in his hand.

"Well, well," says Rudolph, his mouth full of
sausage. "What happened to you? Lost?

Henry turns his head as he hears a sound in the caravan behind him. Elizabeth emerges sleepily. Henry gives a short sardonic laugh.

"Hopelessly lost," he says. "I'm afraid I got off on the wrong road."

Elizabeth looks at him quizzically as we

FADE OUT.

The following day Henry breaks the news to Pas...
and it is most to the Bratislava and getting...
instruments from proper faster — he is going to make
a bride for the monster.

Synopsis of Remaining Sequences of

"THE RETURN OF FRANKENSTEIN"

We see the monster collecting bodies for
Henry, breaking into village funeral parlors at night,
prowling among the marble slabs, discarding bodies not the
proper size.

We see him following a bevy of nuns into
a convent, converting the cloistered quiet into mad pan-
demonium.

Henry begins his new experiment in the
travelling workshop hitherto devoted to the design and
manufacture of puppets. He grows haggard under the strain.
He performs his awful surgery while the spieler for Arnaldo,
the magician, a few yards away, shouts ironically about
sawing a woman in half.

In the interim we advance the sub-plots.
Hans is desolate because he has quarrelled by mail with his
fiancee. Arnaldo has a wife waiting for him in Bratislava
and plans to get rid of Sari before she finds out that her
marriage is not valid. Lothar overhears the situation and
reports it to Sari. In despair Sari seeks advice from
Elizabeth. Seeing Sari disappear in the direction of Henry's
caravan, Arnaldo follows. When Henry refuses to let him in,
Arnaldo accuses him of having Sari inside. Arnaldo goes
for witnesses so that he may accuse Sari of intimacy with
Henry and deny paternity of her unborn child. In the mean-
time Henry rides away with his makeshift laboratory as he
plans to tap the power lines several miles off for the climax of his experiment that night. The monster lopes down
the road behind him.

Henry makes his connections at a transformer station, and with this stolen current causes life to stir in the limbs of the female monster. Through a window the monster is watching the creation of his mate. Then, with a shower of sparks, the current goes off. Henry has short-circuited the power line. Dynamos sputter and lights go out in distant cities. Trouble shooters are dispatched to find the cause of the disturbance.

By a lamp light Henry checks the results of his handiwork. The female monster lives, but Henry confides in Paul that he fears the premature stoppage of the current condemns the experiment to failure.

The approach of the trouble shooters cause Henry and Paul hastily to irradicate traces of their tampering with the power lines. While they are outside, the monster gets into the caravan and runs away with his newly created mate.

Henry and Paul return to the fair grounds, hoping that at last the menace has been definitely lifted from their lives. Their hope is of short duration, however, for the female monster expires while the monster is gleefully rushing her away into the woods. Roaring with disappointed rage, the monster returns to the carnival to wreak havoc. We see the monster on a manical rampage, smashing windows, pulling doors from wagons, and uprooting tent poles. He finds the giantess and drags her by her hair past the animal cages. When Emma tries to interfere, the monster drops the giantess, strangles the lion tamer, and, howling insanely, he tears open the cages of the animals one by one. The lion springs at him. A furious struggle ensues. The lion appears at first to be tearing

the monster to pieces, then the monster gets the upper hand.
We see flashes of the terrified and excited performers and
villagers, gendarmes running with rifles, the sexton ringing
the bell of the village church, and other animals at large.
Now the lion has the monster pinned to the ground. The monster's struggles grow weaker. The lion triumphs.

In a few last anticlimactical scenes we see
the carnival wagons approaching Bratislava in sunshine with
a semblance of a happy ending in the knowledge that Henry and
Elizabeth are at last free from the menace of the monster.

in finishing satisfactorily
all the sub-plots and

Karloff's stand in dummy - Photographer John Mescall and Director James Whale

KARLOFF

THE RETURN OF FRANKENSTEIN

WITH
COLIN CLIVE
MAE CLARKE
EDWARD VAN SLOAN
DWIGHT FRYE

Written by
John L. Balderston

Directed by
James Whale

PRODUCED BY
CARL LAEMMLE JR.

FROM: JOHN BALDERSTON

"THE   RETURN   OF   FRANKENSTEIN

First Rough Draft
June 9, 1934
Revised
June 19th, 1934

"RETURN OF FRANKENSTEIN"

List of Chief Characters

THE MONSTER...Karloff

HENRY FRANENSTEIN..Colin Clive

ELIZABETH, afterwards Henry's wife.......................... Mae Clarke

FATHER GERARD, the village priest.......................Edward Van Sloane

THE MONSTER'S MATE ....Elsa Lanchester ?

FRITZ, The Dwarf, Henry's assistant in lab ....Same man as before

THE BURGOMEISTER OF FRANKENSTEIN ....Same man as before

JUSTINE, an attractive young peasant girl
          servant in the Castle Frankenstein

EDWARD, Young manservant in Castle
          Frankenstein, in love with Justine.

ERIC,   Swiss peasant farmer type, should
          appear not more than thirty.

HILDA, His wife

HERTHA, Their child, a little girl of five,
          who has quite a few lines and must
          be able to act a little

OLD GRANDFATHER, Eric's father, aged blind
                  man, able to play fiddle well,
                  unless his fiddle music is
                  dubbed

PROFESSOR OF ANATOMY, must be able to lecture
                  impressively
                  ****

Minor Characters With Few Lines

BARON FRANKENSTEIN

RUSTIC SCHOOL MASTER

A PEASANT WOMAN

YOUNG RUSTIC YOUTH

YOUNG RUSTIC GIRL

VILLAGE GENDARME

THREE CHARCOAL BURNERS

HALF A DOZEN VILLAGERS, in addition, will have to have
                  two or three lines each.

A-1   MED. SHOT INT. LIVING ROOM
        OF VILLA AT COLIGNY - NIGHT

        On the edge of Lake Geneva,
        in 1816. Furniture, costumes,
        etc., in the period. Mary
        Wollstonecraft Shelley is
        seated by a blazing fire,
        working on a sampler. She
        is an ethereal vision of
        nineteen; her face pale and
        pure, golden hair arranged
        in smooth bands on either
        side of shapely head. Broad
        forehead and earnest nut-
        brown eyes. "Slim and true
        as a Toledo blade".

        Percy Bysshe Shelley, her husband,
        is seated at a desk against
        the wall, a short distance from
        the fire, working with quill pen
        over sheaf of verses. We only
        see his back in this shot, but
        later he is seen as a youth
        of twenty-six, exceptionally
        beautiful, with brilliant blue
        eyes, dark curly hair, and
        a delicate complexion, slender
        build and girlish air. A bundle
        of nerves. His eyes, dreamy
        when at peace, acquire under
        enthusiasm a light almost wild,
        and his voice, usually soft, be-
        comes shrill. His long hair
        floats, his collar opens on his
        girlish throat.

        On the other side of the fire,
        standing at the window, is
        George Gordon Lord Byron, seen
        in profile, his hand raised
        holding back the curtain, as he
        looks out.

        There is a storm over Lake
        Geneva and over the Alps beyond.
        Sheet lightning and distant
        thunder.

        CUT TO:

A-2   LONG SHOT THROUGH WINDOW

        Byron's arm is seen holding
        back curtain; through window
        we can see Lake Geneva and

        CONTINUED:

73

The mountains beyond lit by
lightning flashes, which also
reveal the distant Alps.
Thunder rumbles. Not too
loud - we save our big storm
effects:

CUT TO:

A-3   CLOSE SHOT BYRON AT WINDOW

Lord Byron is twenty-eight;
man of the world in contrast to
the mild looking Shelley; pale
skin, dark blue eyes, black
and slightly curly hair, a
perfect line of eyebrows, nose
and chin firm and well-drawn,
mouth full and voluptuous,
club foot.

                        BYRON
                                (turns from window)
                        Ah, Shelley, come away from
                        those stale verses! Here is
                        Nature in her wildest of moods!
                        Lake Geneva — Mont Blanc -
                        revealed by the lightnings
                        and then blotted out again - -!

As Byron speaks Shelley walks
into camera and stands
beside Byron gazing out of
window.

                        SHELLEY
                        My dear Byron, one night like
                        this is worth the hardships of
                        our trip from England. Those
                        fogs!

                        BYRON
                                (with a grimace)
                        And those people! Those rotten
                        eggs.

                        SHELLEY
                                (looking out at storm)
                        And we poets dare to try to
                        describe such a scene as that!
                        We are as madly arrogant as
                        my wife's Henry Frankenstein!

He turns slightly and
speaks to Mary out of
scene.

                        Mary! Come and see!

CUT TO:

Byron and Shelley at window,
Mary working on sampler by
fire, as before.

                    MARY
                          (lifts her head placidly in
                          response to her husband's
                          remark)
You know, Percy, how lightning
alarms me.
                          (goes on with her stitching)

Byron turns from window.

                    BYRON

                It was just such a night as this
                Mrs. Shelley, when you told us
                your story.

                  MARY

                Not my story - the whole tale
                sprang from the talk between
                two great poets.

                  BYRON
                          (taking few steps forward;
                          his limp now noticeable)
Nonsense! I remember talking
with Shelley about the artificial
creation of life, while you sat
there and never said a word. But
you must not father your dreadful
fable on us.
                          (he limps over and stands
                          in front of Mary and continues
                          half-whimsical, half-serious)
I have shocked all Europe with
my poems - I am driven from my
country and outcast - the world
cunic as George Gordon Lord Byron!
But this girl of nineteen-with the
pure unclouded brow - I swear
to you, Shelley, the night she
red us Henry Frankenstein's
creation of the Monster, I could
not close my eyes!

Mary laughs softly, gently.

CONTINUED:

                              SHELLEY
                                   (turns from window with a
                                   sudden blaze of enthusiasm)
                         Nor I - I saw myself as Henry -
                         afame with his genius, as you
                         Byron, are aflame when you write
                         your verses - and then - after,
                         when in his pride he mocked the
                         Creator of the world - the horror
                         of his success! He would rush
                         away, hoping that the spark he'd
                         kindled in that odious mass of
                         corruption would die of itself!

                              BYRON
                                   (catching Shelley's enthusiasm)
                         Yes! He falls exhausted, after
                         his nights of obscene labor! He
                         wakes! The dead Thing to which
                         he has given life stands at his
                         bedside, looking down on him, with
                         eyes that are alive, yet blank -
                         blank - blank!

                              MARY
                                   (calm and demure, smiles on
                                   the two excited poets)
                         Before I send "Frankenstein" to
                         the publishers, I must work that
                         in, somehow.

                              BYRON
                                   (to Mrs. Shelley)
                         But what excuse have you for
                         inflicting on the public horrors
                         that will bring nightmares to
                         millions of people yet unborn?
                         They censor me - why should you
                         escape?

                              SHELLEY
                                   (springing away from window,
                                   walking up and down the room,
                                   speaking nervously, jerkily)
                         This is no mere tale of horror -
                         it is infused by a great moral
                         idea - man's defiance of God.
                         and his punishment!
                              BYRON
                         Ah, my dear Shelley, you always
                         fun after abstract moral ideas
                         that's why your short poems are
                         your good ones

                              MARY
                                   (smiles at Byron's chaff,
                                   then after pause says re-
                                   flectively)
                         Perhaps to quote Aristotle, the
                         function of stories like
                         Frankenstein is to purge the mind,
                         through pity and terror.

          CUT TO:

A-5   CLOSE SHOT SHELLEY

                    SHELLY
                              (reflectively)
                    'To purge the mind, through
                    pity and terror'
                              (he turns on Mary, speaks
                              violently, shrilly)
                    Mary! That's the weakness of
                    your story - there's no pity!
                    Henry Frankenstein creates this
                    monster - but it never speaks!
                    Your creation scene is a master-
                    piece, but we never get inside
                    the Monster's skin - that's
                    your theme - but you go and burn
                    him up in a mill!

        CUT TO:

A-6   MED. SHOT MARY, SHELLEY,
        BYRON

                    MARY
                              (raising head from her work
                              with a little rippling laugh)
                    Who said he was burned up in a
                    mill?

The two poets look at her
in astonishment.

                    BYRON

                    But you read us the chapter!

                    MARY

                    And you thought that was all?
                    While you have been out on Lake
                    Geneva -
                              (she turns to Byron)
                    you, with your "Childe Harold" -
                              (to Shelley)
                    and you with your "Revolt of
                    Islam" - I have not been idle.
                              (she lays down her needle
                              work on little stool)
                    Shall I tell you the rest of the
                    story of Henry Frankenstein's
                    monster?

                    SHELLEY

                    Yes, yes, it's just the night
                    for a tale like yours - the very
                    air seems full of monsters!

        CONTINUED:

A-6   CONTINUED:

He sinks beside her on the
floor and looks up into
her face, forearm in her
lap. Byron pulls up a chair.

                    BYRON

          Now mind you don't keep me awake
          again, Mary Wollstonecraft Shelley!

Mary looks from one genius to
the other, and laughs a gentle,
girlish laugh, as before.

The screen darkens as the laugh
grows in strength, peal after
peal, until it sounds like the
laugh of devils, and gradually
dies out as we LAP DISSOLVE
SLOWLY INTO the first of a
series of shots from the old
picture.

"THE RETURN OF FRANKENSTEIN"

Screen Play by John L. Balderston

SEQUENCE "A"

The picture opens with a
few quick shots taken from
the climax of the first
picture. We need not exactly
follow the continuity of the
old picture, as no one will
remember this. The idea is
to put across, pictorially,
as briefly as possible, what
happened in the old picture,
so as to avoid much verbal
exposition later.

FROM OLD PICTURE:

A-1   LONG SHOT. .NIGHT. .EXT. MILL

        Peasants milling about its
        base with torches, fire
        running up the mill.

        CUT TO:

A-2   INT. MILL

        Monster chasing Henry
        Frankenstein in top of
        mill. Monster seizes
        Henry.

A-3   LONG SHOT BURNING MILL
        FROM BELOW

        Monster appears on balcony
        carrying the unconscious
        Henry. He hurls the body
        down.

        CUT TO:

A-4   MED. SHOT. .CIRCLING ARMS
        OF WINDMILL

        Henry's body caught on one
        of them. The arms turn and
        his body crashes to the ground.

                        PEASANTS (horrified cries)
                            Henry! Henry Frankenstein!
                            He's killed!

        (NOTE: New sound needed
        her over the old shot

        CUT TO:

A-5   MED. SHOT...HENRY'S
        BODY ON GROUND

        Peasants rush to him and
        start to pick him up

        CUT TO:

A-6   FULL SHOT..BURNING
        MILL

        The fire now raging
        throughout the structure,
        a great torch of flame.

        CUT TO:

A-7   INT. TOP OF MILL
        MED▢ SHOT

        The Monster, mad with
        terror, is hemmed in by
        flames and is dashing
        about.

        CUT TO:

A-8   INT. TOP OF MILL

        Huge beam has crashed
        down. Monster lies
        crushed underneath.

        CUT TO:

A-8A   INT. TOP OF MILL...
        CLOSE SHOT

        Monster pinned under
        beams, flames come
        through floor and lap
        around him.

        (NOTE: The above is
        the last shot taken from
        the old film).

        CUT TO:

A-9   EXT. MILL...FULL SHOT
        (MINIATURE?)

        The whole structure is
        a roaring furnace, and
        we see it collapse.

        LAP DISSOLVE TO:

A-10   EXTRA LONG SHOT. .NIGHT

Group of peasants stand-
ing on rocky ledge in
foreground watching the
dying fire of the burning
mill, seen at a longer
distance than before, have
sunk into a mass from which
a few flickering flames
still come, but the fire is
almost out, which, with the
lap dissolve, indicates that
several hours have passed.

CUT TO:

A-11   MED. SHOT. . .GROUP OF
        PEASANTS

watching fire. Two or
three of them turn and
trudge out of scene, off
for home. Three linger
behind, dimly silhouetted
against the night sky.
They speak in low, shaken
voices, still aghast from
the terrible happenings
of the night.

                    1st PEASANT
                It wa'nt human, it wa'nt
                human - eight feet tall,
                it was!

            2nd PEASANT
                Master Henry Frankenstein
                murdered on his bridal
                night!
                        (stops, shakes head)
                That poor Mistress Elizabeth!

            3rd PEASANT
                There's a devil lives in
                the Jura Mountains - up
                in the ice - maybe that's
                what it was - -

            2nd PEASANT   (interrupting)
                Lives in ice, maybe, but
                no man, no devil, could
                live in that fire.

            1st PEASANT   (doggedly)
                Ain't there devils in
                hell? Ain't you heard
                Father Gerard preach about
                the fires in hell?

                    (CONTINUED)

81

                    2nd PEASANT
                            (shaking his head,
                            sadly)
                    Poor Master Henry. Killed
                    on his bridal night

CAMERA PULLS BACK as
another figure toils up
towards the men along the
ridge, Father
Gerald, the village Cure.
He wears a Priest's hat
and cassock. The peasants
recognize him.

                    1st PEASANT
                            Father Gerard!

They all bow awkwardly
as Father Gerard reaches
them and raises his hand
in blessing.

                    1st PEASANT
                            T'was need we had for a
                            priest, Father, for this
                            night's work.

                    FATHER GERARD
                            Where are Baron Frankenstein
                            and the Herr Burgomeister?

                    2nd PEASANT   (pointing)
                            The Burgomeister was over
                            yonder but now, watching
                            the fire.

                    FATHER GERARD
                            (as he starts to move
                            off)
                            I have just left Henry
                            Frankenstein. Through
                            God's mercy, he will live.

Murmurs of joy from the
peasants.

                    1st PEASANT
                            (crossing himself)
                            May God be praised!

As Father Gerard toils
out of scene across rock,

CUT TO:

A-12   MED. SHOT..ANOTHER PART OF
        THE MOUNTAIN..NIGHT

Father Gerard and the
Burgomaster are conversing
in low tones.   (CONTINUED)

                         FATHER GERARD
                              Terribly shaken - a few
                              bones broken, but Henry
                              Frankenstein is in no
                              danger, Herr Burgomeister.
                              The doctor assured me of it.
                         BURGOMASTER
                                   (crossing himself)
                              A miracle! And the fiend
                              himself has died as he
                              deserved - does Henry know
                              that?
                         FATHER GERARD
                              He has been told. But
                              where is his father?
                         BURGOMASTER
                              The Baron came back after
                              they carried his son home -
                              I think he's over beyond
                              the mill.

CAMERA MOVES BACK
taking in three other
peasants who have been
standing gazing, listen-
ing. Father Gerard now
waves them back, for what
he has to say to the
Burgomaster is confidential.
The others withdraw and
Father Gerard continues:

                         FATHER GERARD
                              Henry's body will recover - -
                              but these horrors have
                              affected his mind. This
                              creature you have burned
                              in the mill - Poor Henry
                              says that it is not a man.
                              "I made it with my own
                              hands, Father," he told
                              me. "Out of the corpse of
                              a dead peasant, using the
                              brain of a criminal" - While
                              Elizabeth holds his hand and
                              soothes his brow, he keeps
                              repeating insane blasphemies:
                              "I created life in man's
                              image - and made myself
                              equal to God".

                         BURGOMASTER   (shaking head)
                              His studies in anatomy have
                              turned his brain - but who
                              could the creature be? An
                              escaped madman?

                         FATHER GERARD
                              Henry fears the fiend to
                              whom he thinks he gave life
                              has not died in the fire.
                              He made me promise to return
                              and make sure.
                                        (CONTINUED)

83

                              BURGOMASTER
                                   (pointing with his
                                   hand)
                              What living thing could
                              survive that furnace?
                              There's nothing left but
                              charred beams and embers.
                         FATHER GERARD
                              At least we can search
                              and set Henry's mind at
                              rest. And if there are
                              remains, my duty as a
                              priest . . .

                         BURGOMASTER   (interrupting)
                              No Christian burial for
                              that murderer, in God's name,
                              Father!
                         FATHER GERARD
                              God is love. Man's justice
                              has been done, it is not
                              for us to judge further.
                         BURGOMASTER
                              Have it your own way. At
                              least we can look. There
                              may be something left.

He beckons to the group
of peasants, who draw
near as he motions to
them.

                              BURGOMASTER
                              Come with us. I want you
                              to search the ruins for
                              the body.

He beckons to the group
of peasants, who draw
near as he motions to
them.

                              BURGOMASTER
                              Come with us. I want you
                              to search the ruins for
                              the body.

The group moves off, some
carrying torches.
CUT TO:

A-13   MED. FULL SHOT . .SMOKING
        RUINS. .OF MILL. .NIGHT

The mill has collapsed into
a heap of charred timbers.
Smoke still curls up, but
peasants, in pulling debris
about looking for the Monster's
body, disturb embers and send
showers of sparks up.

Half a dozen men, dimly seen
by the flare of the torches,
are working in the debris
while Father Gerard and the
Burgomaster direct the search.
CUT TO:

A-14   MEDIUM CLOSE HHOT..
        PEASANT

        Tugging at a large
        beam. He moves it,
        stumbles, shrieks and
        disappears as though
        he had fallen into some
        trap beneath.

        CUT TO:

A-15   FLASH SHOT. .FALLING BODY

        Plunging down through some
        sort of circular pit. When
        the peasant removed the
        large beam this allowed a
        shaft of moonlight to filter
        through the hole. The pit
        is faced with rough, slimy
        stones.

        CUT TO:

A-16   MEDIUM CLOSE SHOT -
        BOTTOM OF WELL

        The peasant plunges into
        water, which is covered with
        green slime. Floating on the
        surface are charred bits of
        wood. One large beam,
        scarred by fire, has fallen
        down the pit and stands up-
        right at an angle in the
        water, one edge wedged
        against the moist stones
        of the well. The beam is
        some twelve feet long.
        This is the beam under which
        we saw the Monster apparently
        trapped above about to be
        burned to death.

        The peasant's head reappears
        on the surface of the water.
        He grabs at the beam for
        support.

        CUT TO:

A-17   CLOSE SHOT. .SURFACE OF WATER

        Peasant is holding onto beam,
        only his head and arms visible
        above the water. Over the
        beam now appears, slowly,
        another head. It is that of
        the Monster. Green slime from
        the water is caked in his hair.

        As the peasant sees this
        horrible face appear he
        screams with terror. The

                                        (CONTINUED)

                        85

A-17   CONTINUED

        Monster gives a kind
        of rattle of rage, hate
        and triumph in his throat,
        the CAMERA KEEPING ON THE
        MONSTER'S FACE.

        The monster pulls himself
        up, resting the middle
        part of his body on the
        beam until he has his hands
        and arms free.

        The peasant screams again
        with terror, but cannot
        let go of the beam as this
        is all that saves him from
        drowning.

        The monster slowly raises
        his arms and brings his
        great hands around the
        peasant's neck. The
        peasant's screams die into
        a gurgle as the monster
        with one shake, breaks
        loose the peasant's hold
        on the beam and presses
        his head down under the
        green slime on the surface.

        CUT TO:

A-18   CLOSEUP. .MONSTER'S FACE

        Seen in the moonlight,
        uttering hoarse cries
        of rage as he holds his
        victim under the water.

        CUT TO:

A-19   MED. SHOT . . .INT. WELL

        Shooting up from the
        surface of the water.
        The top of the well is
        partly closed by charred
        beams and debris from the
        collapse of the timbers of
        the mill, but open enough
        to allow a shaft of moon-
        light and a glimpse of
        stars.
        The huge, ungainly form
        of the monster, more mis-
        shapen and weird than ever
        as seen from this distorted
        angle, is crawling up towards
        the top, using the side of
        the beam and the slimy stones
        of the well for support,
        clinging with his fingers to
        the interstices between the
        stones. The monster's   (CONTINUED)

86

A-19   CONTINUED

        clothing is partly
        burned. He gives little
        moans and sobs and rattles
        of pain, drawn from him
        by his burns.

        CUT TO:

A-20   TOP OF WELL SHAFT. .
        MED. SHOT

        The Burgomaster, Father
        Gerard and the other
        peasants are frantically
        pulling away timbers trying
        to find what happened to the
        man who dropped through, and
        to rescue him.

                        FATHER GERARD
                                (shouting down the
                                hole)
                        It's all right, Hans, help
                        is coming! We'll get you
                        up!

        As these things are said
        the peasants are pulling
        away timbers, enlarging
        the hole. Now the Burgo-
        master holds his torch
        over the hole and he and
        Father Gerard peer down.

        CUT TO:

A-21   INT. WELL SHAFT. .CLOSE SHOT

        Shooting from the top as
        through the eyes of Father
        Gerard and Burgomaster.

        The monster's great head
        and shoulders are now seen
        near the top as he pulls
        himself up. The two men at
        the top shrink back at what
        they see.

        CUT TO:

A-22   INT. WELL SHAFT. .CLOSE SHOT

        Shooting up from half way
        down. The Burgomaster's
        cry of terror come through
        the cut as the monster
        toiling upwards, answers
        with a roar of defiance.

        A flaming torch, dropped
        by the scared Burgomaster,
        falls past the monster
        lighting up his whole body.   (CONTINUED)

A-22   CONTINUED

        The torch plunges down
        into the water where it is
        extinguished with a hiss.

        CUT TO:

A-23   EXT. MOUTH OF WELL
        MOONLIGHT....MED. SHOT

        The Burgomaster, whose torch
        dropped down the well, is
        scrambling away through the
        ruins over burned timbers,
        as he cries in terror:

                              BURGOMASTER
                         It's down there - it's
                         alive - it's coming up -
                         save yourselves

        The other peasants, with
        torches, who have been
        searching in the debris for
        the monster's body, utter
        cries of alarm and scramble
        after the Burgomaster. Only
        Father Gerard, holding his
        torch, stand his ground near
        the mouth of the well

        CUT TO:

A-24   CLOSE SHOT..MOUTH OF WELL..
        MOONLIGHT..

        The monster's head and
        shoulders emerge. The
        monster painfully pulls him-
        self out.

        While he is dressed as in the
        last shot of the old picture,
        his clothes and body are
        badly burned. One side of
        his face is scorched. As he
        pulls himself out he sees the
        Priest. Here is one of his
        enemies. All men are his
        enemies. He glares at him,
        rage and murder in his face,
        and gives inarticulate animal-
        like cries as he stretches
        out his arms and shambles
        toward Father Gerard.

        CUT TO:

A-25   MED. CLOSE SHOT..FATHER
        GERARD AND MONSTER

        Still holding torch,
        Father Gerard drops to his
        knees and begins to mumble

                                        (CONTINUED)

prayers. The monster
stumbles up to him,
but stops. The monster by
now has a wholesome fear
of fire and the Priest's
torch saves him from being
attacked

Whimpering from the agony
of his burns, which hurt more
now that he is out of the water,
the Monster turns and shambles
off out of the debris, CAMERA
ON his back.

CUT TO:

A-26   MED. SHOT..MOONLIGHT ...
LOOKING DOWN THE MOUNTAIN

From the ruins. The monster's
receding back is seen as he
scrambles down.

CUT TO:

A-27   MED. SHOT..LEDGE OF ROCK..
MOONLIGHT...

The monster's vast hulk
comes over ledge and with
abnormal agility, he scrambles
down and hurries by CAMERA.

CUT TO:

A-28   ROCKY PATH AT FOOT OF
MOUNTAIN...MOONLIGHT...
MED. SHOT...

Baron Frankenstein, attended
by a villager with a torch,
is stumbling down the rocky
path. The monster's cries
of rage and pain are heard as
he approaches. The men turn,
looking back.

            PEASANT   (in panic, to Baron)
               It's coming, Baron

The Baron turns as if to
face the oncoming monster.
The peasant grabs his arm to
hurry him away.

            PEASANT
               Come, Baron Frankenstein!
               That thing has the strength
               of twenty men!

            BARON
               Stand by with the torch!
                           (CONTINUED)

                         BARON   (Cont'd)
                              Let me see this lunatic
                              that tried to kill my son!
                              Moral courage is all you
                              need to deal with madmen.
                              You're all a pack of
                              cowards!

The monster's bellow is
heard closer, and now the
Baron's one protection is
removed by the cowardly
peasant, who turns and flees
with the torch.

                         BARON   (shouting after him)
                              Come back with that torch!

But the peasant pays no
heed, and in the semi-
darkness the monster
bursts into the CAMERA
upon the Baron.

With a snarl, the monster
clasps a huge hand around
the old man's neck. One
wrench and the Baron's
neck is broken, and the
monster tosses the lifeless
body aside, and continues
plunging down path and out
of CAMERA.

(NOTE: The Baron should
never be seen closely or in
any light that will show his
face. All we need then is an
actor who looks vaguely like
Fred Kerr, and has a voice not
too unlike him for his few
lines. We must introduce the
Baron only to kill him off,
since we have to play a few
scenes in the Frankenstein
Castle with the same characters
in the old film, where the Baron
was all over the place. Also
the Baron's death has a value
for next sequence in increasing
Henry's remorse and horror)

CUT TO:

A-29   EDGE OF LAKE..MED. SHOT...
        MOONLIGHT...

The monster, still crying
from pain, and rubbing his
burns, stumbles into CAMERA.
He sees the water. He stumbles
into the lake and throws
himself down in the shallow
water, to ease the pain of
his burns.
DISSOLVE TO:

B-1   MED. SHOT...HENRY FRANKENSTEIN'S
       BEDROOM IN THE CASTLE FRANKENSTEIN
       ...(DAY)

       Henry is lying asleep in bed,
       his left hand stretched out
       holding Elizabeth's right hand.

       Elizabeth, Henry's fiancee, is
       sitting beside bed in chair, in
       a cramped position, looking ex-
       hausted.

       Justine, a young maidservant,
       wearing band of crepe in mourn-
       ing for the dead Baron, approach-
       es the bed and indicates in dumb
       show concern and anxiety for
       Elizabeth. She shows by her ges-
       tures that she is urging Eliza-
       beth to take her hand out of the
       sleeping Henry's handclasp and
       come away from the bed. But
       Elizabeth lays her finger on the
       maid's lips as Justine bends
       down to whisper to Elizabeth,
       forbidding the maid to make any
       sound that will waken Henry. The
       maid shakes her head sadly as
       she stretches up and turns away.

       CUT TO:

B-2   BEDROOM DOOR...MED. SHOT

       It opens and Edward, a young
       manservant in livery, also wear-
       ing crepe, enters with a bowl
       of steaming broth on a tray.
       Justine comes up to him, shaking
       her head and putting her finger
       to her lips. Edward looks at
       Henry and Elizabeth, then turns
       and goes out, followed by Jus-
       tine, who closes the door gently,
       leaving it unlatched to make no
       sound.

       CUT TO:

B-3   MED. SHOT...HALLWAY
       ...OUTSIDE HENRY'S DOOR

Justine and Edward, who still
carries the tray, are talking
in agitated and low tones.

(NOTE: These two servants are
introduced here, not merely
for exposition, but because
they both have important roles
to play in Sequence 'F'.)

                         EDWARD
                    A man don't get well by
                    starving to death! He
                    ought to be waked up -
                    three nights and two days
                    it's been since it hap-
                    pened, Justine, and in
                    that time he's not touched
                    food.

                    JUSTINE
                    It's sleep he needs, the
                    doctor said.

                    EDWARD
                    He's had plenty. Twelve
                    hours he's not opened his
                    eyes...

                    JUSTINE   (wiping away senti-
                                  mental tear)
                    And Mistress Elizabeth's
                    hand!
                            (sententiously)
                    That's love, Edward, that
                    is.

                    EDWARD
                    What's love?

                    JUSTINE
                    Ain't I just told you?
                    For twelve hours she's
                    never moved - her arm
                    stretched out on that bed,
                    numbed as ice by now, no
                    feeling in it.

                    EDWARD   (nods)
                    If I was holding your hand,
                    and the doctor said I wasn't
                    to be waked up, would you
                    do that for me?

                    JUSTINE
                    Not if twenty ice devils
                    came down from the glaciers,
                    and threw you from off the
                    top of twenty mills on fire,
                    I wouldn't

        (CONTINUED)

                           92

B-3   (CONTINUED)

Edward is a solemn youth, who
doesn't understand kidding,
and looks at her rather sadly,
as he stands holding his tray.
So she makes up to him with a
little laugh, a chuck under the
chin, and a kiss.

                    EDWARD
                    How can you laugh in this
                    house, with the poor Baron
                    not cold in his grave?

CUT TO:

B-4   INT. HENRY'S BEDROOM
       ...CLOSE SHOT

Henry, asleep in the bed, is
still holding Elizabeth's hand.
She sits there watching him,
tensely, anxiously. Henry
stirs a little and tosses to
one side, muttering as though
in nightmare.

                    HENRY
                    Devil - fiend - assassin -
                    Let me go!

He makes a sound as though
strangling and struggles in
the bed. Elizabeth places her
other hand on his brow. He
wakes. He gives a half sob as
he sees her anxious face bending over him.

                    HENRY
                    Elizabeth - my love - thank
                    God, your face! Your face -
                    not that face!

                    ELIZABETH
                        (trying to soothe him)
                    You've had a good long sleep,
                    Henry darling. Now if you'll
                    only stop worrying about
                    these horrors that are all
                    over -

                    HENRY   (unheeding her and
                            interrupting)
                    It's day! How long have I
                    slept? Is there no more news?
                    No more murders, no more
                    blood on my hands? Dr. Waldman
                    killed - and then the little
                    girl - and that villager -
                    and my father - and it's only
                    beginning! Is the monster im-
                    mortal? How could it have es-
                    caped from that fire?

(CONTINUED)

93

                              ELIZABETH
                                   Henry, you told Father
                                   Gerard how you made this
                                   thing out of dead bodies,
                                   and brought it to life - -
                                   That was wrong of you - you
                                   musn't speak of it - only
                                   you and I and Victor know
                                   the truth.

                              HENRY
                                   Gerard is a priest - my
                                   confessor - I must ask
                                   pardon from God - I must
                                   have absolution.

                              ELIZABETH
                                   I know - but he didn't be-
                                   lieve you. He thinks your
                                   studies in these strange
                                   science ...

                              HENRY   (hysterically)
                                   I thin I am mad. Not mad
                                   the way they think I am.
                                   But the thought of this
                                   thing that I made with my
                                   own hands, breathed life
                                   into, turn into a devil,
                                   turned loose on the world
                                   to murder innocent victims
                                   ...

                              ELIZABETH
                                   Please, Henry, please. You
                                   mustn't talk now. Edward
                                   has been keeping some broth
                                   hot for you - you've had
                                   nothing.

As she speaks she tries to
raise her left hand to pull
the bell-rope beside the bed
to summon the servants, but
her arm is numb and she can't
lift it, so she shifts and
pulls the bell-rope with her
right hand. Henry doesn't notice this bit of business.

CUT TO:

B-5   MED. SHOT...DOOR
        ...HENRY'S BEDROOM

The door opens and Justine
comes in, followed by Edward
with the tray. Justine runs
to her mistress, bending over
her, putting an arm around
her to help her up.

(CONTINUED)

B-5   (CONTINUED)

> Elizabeth rises, stiffly, with
> difficulty, staggers and al-
> most collapses from exhaustion
> and cramp, but Justine holds
> her.

                    HENRY
              What's the matter, Eliza-
              beth?

                    ELIZABETH
              Nothing. I'm all right.

> Justine, as she speaks to
> Henry, a speech which Eliza-
> beth vainly tries to stop,
> lifts Elizabeth's numb left
> arm and rubs it vigorously.

                    JUSTINE
              You ought to know, Master
              Henry. For twelve solid
              hours she's sat here beside
              the bed and kept hand
              in yours, so's she wouldn't
              wake you by pulling it away.

              HENRY   (tears starting to
                         his eyes)
              Elizabeth, you're not a
              woman - you're an angel -
              I don't deserve ...

     CUT TO:

B-6   CLOSE UP...EDWARD

              EDWARD   (solemnly)
              That's love.

     CUT TO:

B-7   MED. SHOT...GROUP...BY BED
       ..HENRY.. ELIZABETH AND
       JUSTINE

                    ELIZABETH
              Hush, Henry. The doctor
              said we must not wake you
              for food or anything if you
              were asleep - and, thank
              God, you did sleep.

> During this speech Justine has
> continued to rub Elizabeth's
> arm,

                    ELIZABETH
              Than you, Justine, my dear.

> She bends her arm, which
> Justine has been rubbing, and
> turns to Edward, who still has
> the tray with the broth.

(CONTINUED)

She speaks to Henry as she
takes the broth from the
tray.

                    ELIZABETH
                        See, my arm is all right.

She kneels by the bed with
the broth and holds it to
Henry's lips. As he drinks
she speaks to the servants.

                    ELIZABETH
                        Go and get some rest now,
                        children.
                            (to Henry)
                        Dear, faithful Justine and
                        Edward - they've not had a
                        wink of sleep since it hap-
                        pened.

As she speaks the servants go
out of scene.

                    HENRY   (to Elizabeth)
                        You've talked with the
                        doctor - how long does he
                        think ...

                    ELIZABETH
                          (gently)
                        I must be your nurse for a
                        few weeks, Henry.

                    HENRY   (violently)
                        No! You must go! You must
                        leave this accursed house!

                    ELIZABETH
                          (her hand on his head)
                        Your father is taken from
                        you, Henry - - you are alone
                        now in Castle Frankenstein.
                        This monster broke up our
                        wedding - and as soon as
                        you're well enough, Father
                        Gerard will make me your
                        wife.

                    HENRY   (with bitter hysterical
                                laughter)
                        My wife! You'd marry a man
                        who murdered his father?
                        These deaths I must answer
                        for - and how many more? How
                        many more to come?

                    ELIZABETH
                          (trying to soothe him)
                        When you brought that dead
                        thing to life, Henry, you
                        did what any man would do,
                        if he had your genius. You're
                        not to blame. You could not
                        foresee ...

(CONTINUED)

                              HENRY   (interrupting -
                                            now raving)
                          Pride! "By that sin fell
                          the Angels"! I thought my-
                          self equal to God. God
                          created life in man and
                          beast! Why couldn't I?
                          I did it! You saw me do
                          it! Blasphemy! And this
                          is my punishment. The curse
                          of Cain is on me - but how-
                          ever low I am, do you think
                          that I could let you link
                          your life to mine?
                                  (he sits up in bed
                                   as she vainly tries
                                   to make him lie back
                                   on his pillow)
                          No! I have one task, one
                          thing left in life, to seek
                          out this creature and de-
                          stroy him - that's the only
                          atonement possible - and if
                          he destroys me, perhaps I can
                          win peace beyond the grave -
                          there is none for me in this
                          world -

Unable to restrain Henry's
raving, Elizabeth sinks on
the floor and buries her head
in the bedclothes, sobbing
wildly.

DISSOLVE INTO:

DISSOLVE IN:

C-1   MED. SHOT FOOTHILLS OF THE
JURA MOUNTAINS - DAY - AUTUMN

A small wood of straggling
pines. The monster staggers
in. He is famished, desperate
for food. He sinks on all
fours, pulls up some stones,
eagerly seeking for beetles
or any crawling things that
will stay his hunger. He
scoops up something from
under a rock with his hand
and stuffs it into his mouth.
He then rises and shambles
on.

CUT TO:

C-2   MED. SHOT BACKWATER IN SMALL
RIVER

It is still water, branches
and plants hang close to the
surface. We see two or three
lazy muskrats, their tails
flapping characteristically
in the water.

The monster's face appears
through the foliage, greed
and hunger registered on
his face as he sees possible
food. His face is withdrawn.

CUT TO:

C-3   CLOSE SHOT MONSTER BY
SMALL TREE

With one wrench of
his superhumanly powerful
arm he splinters a branch
from the tree, making a
formidable club.

CUT TO:

C-4   MED. SHOT BACKWATER, AS BEFORE

One muskrat is flapping near
bank. The monster leaps into
the water and with a blow of
his club violent enough to
kill an ox, he kills the
muskrat. He drops club
and his greedy hands pick
up muskrat, carrying it to
his mouth.

CUT TO:

C-5   CLOSE SHOT FOREST - DAY

Monster, after having finished
the raw muskrat, flings
skin and tail, all that is
left, down on the ground and
looks about in quest of further
food, his ravenous hunger un-
appeased.

CUT TO:

C-6   MED. SHOT CHARCOAL BURNER'S
        CAMP...TWILIGHT

Three rough woodsmen, their
work for the day over, are
sitting around a fire. The
utensils of their trade have
been heaped to one side, and
they are all eagerly watching
a wild pig roasting in the
embers of the fire.

The charcoal burner who killed
this unusual treat has his
rifle beside him. The three
men are all greedily intent
in the roasting process.

                        1st CHARCOAL BURNER

                    Been half a year since I tasted
                    roast pig.

                    2ND CHARCOAL BURNER
                        (chaffing the third)

                    A lucky shot! Fifty meters,
                    with that old gun - -

(CONTINUED)

99

                              3RD CHARCOAL BURNER
                                   (fondling gun affectionately)

                              Ay, fifty meters, and a wild pig
                              runs fast, and the light was bad.
                              Luck, you call it? Give me a
                              shot like that every day, and
                              every night we'll sup on roast
                              meat. Pull it out of the fire
                              Hans.

                              1ST CHARCOAL BURNER
                                   (greedily smacking lips)

                              Yes, 'tis ready, mates.

He rises to his knees, picks
up pair of iron tongs used
in charcoal burning and
starts pulling roast pig
out of fire.

As he does so the second
charcoal burner hears sound
off, and looks up, startled

                              2ND CHARCOAL BURNER

                              What might that be?

Now the monster's inarticulate
growl is heard off. The third
charcoal burner rises with his
gun. They all look off.

CUT TO:

C-7   EDGE OF LITTLE CLEARING
       AS SEEN BY FIRELIGHT
       MED. LONG SHOT.

       The monster, attracted by the
       firelight and sound of voices,
       is seen shambling towards the
       men. Cries of fear from the
       Charcoal burners come over the
       sound track.

       CUT TO:

C-8   MED. SHOT BESIDE FIRE

       The three charcoal burners
       are terrified at the appalling
       creature advancing upon them.
       The man with the gun half rises
       it with wobbling hands, but
       his companions have already fled.
       He glances after them, drops the
       gun and runs out of scene lea-
       ving his cloak on the ground.

       (CONTINUED)

C-8   (CONTINUED)

       The monster enters scene
       stands beside the fire,
       looking after the three men,
       The sound of their retreat
       through the bushes dies out.
       The Monster looks down at the
       roast pig. He kneels. He
       touches the pig. It burns
       his hand. He rises, anger in
       his face, and boots the pig,
       kicking it away from the fire.
       As it is tender and roasted per-
       fectly, his boot splits it open.
       His action shows that he con-
       siders the meat has been spoiled
       by the fire. He stands looking
       down at the shattered roast pig.

       CUT TO:

C-9   CLOSEUP MONSTER.

       showing rage and disappointment.
       He puts his burned finger in his
       mouth, and suddenly a new ex-
       pression comes into his face.
       He likes the taste. His nostrils
       now distend. He sniffs. He
       smells the delicious odor of
       roast pig for the first time.

C-10   CLOSE SHOT ROAST PIG.

       on the ground. The Monster
       kneels into camera and picks
       up a chunk of meat, which
       comes apart in his hands
       and smells it. A slow smile
       of pleasure overspreads his
       face. Then he takes a bite
       thinking that if it smells like
       this, perhaps even if it was in
       the fire it is worth trying.
       As he gets the succulent flavor
       the smile becomes beatific.
       Raw meat was never like this.
       Now he begins to wolf the
       meat down, seizing the whole
       carcass and burying his
       head in it. He has learned
       one of the virtues of fire.

       CUT TO:

C-11   MED. SHOT GROUP OF TREES
        NIGHT.

        The fire of the Charcoal
        Burners is seen, too far
        away for warmth to reach the
        trees. The Monster enters,
        wiping his mouth with the
        back of his great hand. He
        carries the thin cloak left
        by the charcoal burner. He
        has gorged himself to repletion.
        He yawns. After food, sleep.
        He lies down beside tree.
        There is frost on the ground.
        It is cold, his teeth chatter.
        He tries to huddle up and
        get some warmth out of the
        burned rags that he wears, and
        the thin cloak, but he suffers
        from the cold. He moans. He
        sits up and looks at the fire,
        which is too far away for
        warmth to reach him. The fire
        which nearly killed him was too
        hot, but some sort of rudiment-
        tary idea as to heat and cold
        percolates his mind as he looks
        at the fire. He rises and
        starts toward it.

        CUT TO:

C-12   MED. SHOT. FIRE.

        It has burned down, but
        still gives out plenty of
        warmth. The monster enters
        scene and approaches it
        gingerly. First, he shows
        fear of it. He doesn't want
        to be burned again, but he
        stretches out his hands to
        the warmth. He lies down
        again to sleep, this time
        warmed by the heat. He
        sighs with contentment. He
        has learned another use of
        fire.

        DISSOLVE TO:

DISSOLVE IN:

C-13   MED. SHOT. FOREST. DAY

An alarmed rabbit, or other
small animal, scurries across
screen, followed by a large
stone, which misses the rabbit.
Rabbit disappears in underbrush
at top speed.

CUT TO:

C-14   CLOSE SHOT. MONSTER

with right arm extended
having just thrown the stone.
He drops his arm and his
face works convulsively with
disappointment. He turns,
looks about him, strips a
few berries off bush with
his huge paw, gathering twigs
as well as berries, and munches
mouth full. He staggers on into
the woods.

CUT TO:

C-15   MED. SHOT. A SMALL STREAM

The monster enters and
sees the water. He is con-
sumed with thirst and lum-
bers to stream as quickly as
possible, throws himself
on his stomach, drinking
eagerly and greedily.

CUT TO:

C-16   CLOSE SHOT. MONSTER. DRINKING

He raises his head, and as he
looks into the stream a startled
expression comes into his face.
He is seeing himself for the
first time mirrored in the
pool.

CUT TO:

C-17   CLOSEUP REFLECTION

in pool of Monster's horrible
face.

CUT TO:

C-18   CLOSEUP MONSTER

His face is contoured with
a mixture of rage and self-
pity. Now, perhaps, he under-
stands for the first time how
different he is from other
men, and why they hate and
fear him and flee from him,
or try to kill him. He re-
gisters this by tearing out
a stone from bank and angrily
shattering his reflection
in the water as he rises and
hurls stone into it.

CUT TO:

C-19   MINIATURE SHOT SMALL VILLAGE

in valley. Smoke is rising
from the cottages of the
peasants. There are some
twenty houses on one winding
street.

CUT TO:

C-21   INT. PEASANT'S COTTAGE
        DAY...MED. SHOT

        in the one room of their
        humble abode, an old man
        and his wife are sitting down
        to their frugal midday meal.
        There is some cheese on the
        table, a large loaf of Swiss
        black bread, some raw vegetables
        and a firkin of wine. The wo-
        man looks toward the door and
        suddenly horror comes into
        her eyes and she screams. The
        man looks up and registers
        astonishment and alarm.

        CUT TO:

C-22   MED. CLOSE SHOT. MONSTER

        standing in doorway. He
        points with his hand to
        table with food, and then
        to his mouth.

        There is no menace in the
        Monster's attitude toward
        these people. He is simply
        hungry. We must make clear
        throughout that his savagery
        and murder evolve from what
        people do to him, and not
        from an innate viciousness.
        His mood was murderous in
        the fire scene because he
        wanted revenge on Henry and
        the villagers who tried to
        kill him, and was maddened
        by pain when he got out of the
        well.

        CUT TO:

C-23   MED. SHOT. INT. ROOM

        The old woman screams and
        rushes out back door. The
        man climbs through the window.
        As they disappear the Monster
        goes to table and greedily
        begins to wolf the food.
        He sees the firkin of wine
        picks it up and takes a drink.

C-24   CLOSE SHOT. MONSTER DRINKING

He puts down the wine and smacks
his lips. He likes his first
drink of something stronger
than water. He drinks again,
a long pull. Then he rams some
cheese and a huge hunk of black
bread into his mouth and chews
vigorously. He takes a third
drink of wine. As he is drinking, the wine. As he is drinking the wine jug tilted up
above his head,

CUT TO:

C-25   MED. LONG SHOT. VILLAGE
STREET. DAY.

A small group of people
surrounding the old man
and woman who fled from
the house. They are chatter-
ing excitedly and pointing
up the street towards camera.
Other villagers hurry from
all directions to see what
the excitement is about.

CUT TO:

C-24   MED. SHOT EXCITED GROUP OF
20 or 30 VILLAGERS.

Men, women and children, all
talking at once. In the
foreground of the crowd are
the old man and woman, and
the town constable dressed in
old-fashioned skirted uniform
with triangular hat. He
seems to be interrogating the
old couple, but there is too
much noise for more than a
few isolated sentences to be
audible. Among the ad libs
we hear

                    VILLAGERS

        The wild man from Belrive...
        Four murders.....
        Killed Old Baron Frankenstein
        Ten feet tall.....
        Uglier than Satan.....
        He can take a man's head in
        his great hand and crush his
        skull......

(CONTINUED)

C-26   (CONTINUED)

CAMERA NOW FAVORS a woman who
gathers her two children to
her, one under each arm,
screaming:

                    WOMAN
                    The devil himself! It is --
                    the ice devil from the mountains!
                         (she starts dragging the
                         children away, calling to
                         a man, evidently her husband)
                    Come Albrecht, bar the doors and
                    windows!

This incident is typical
of the panic on the part
of some of the villagers
but others are belligerent.
Men and boys begin picking
up stones. Dogs bark. The
Constable is heard shouting:

                    CONSTABLE
                    Get your guns, men!

CUT TO:

C-27   INT. PEASANT'S HOME
         MED. SHOT.

The monster has finished
both the food and the wine.
He holds jug upsidedown
but there is no more. He
gets up and moves unsteadily,
legs shaky from the drink, a-
cross room towards front door.

CUT TO:

C-28   VILLAGE STREET. MED. SHOT

The braver villagers are in
a group ready to do battle
to the invader. The Constable
now has his gun, and old-fashioned blunderbuss of the type still
seen in Swiss villages. Two or
three other men have guns, others
have clubs, the boys have stones.
The Constable is giving orders:

(CONTINUED)

C-28   (CONTINUED)

                              CONSTABLE
                        Thowald - and you - and you....

As he speaks he seizes
each villager he addresses
by the shoulder.

                              CONSTABLE

                        Go up through the alley, come out
                        into the street above the house
                        if he tries to break back that
                        way shoot - and mind you don't
                        miss.

The three men,two with
guns and one with a club,
go off up into a side alley.

CUT TO:

C-29   EXT. PEASANT'S HOUSE. MED.
        SHOT.

        The monster appears in the
        doorway, then he shambles
        out into the street. The
        wine has made him pleased
        with himself and with life.
        Also distinctly tipsy, and
        he stumbles. But it has made
        him feel no more an outcast.
        He even grins. It is a ghastly
        grin, that makes him look even
        more horrible than before.

        As the CAMERA KEEPS ON HIM
        and he walks out into the
        middle of the street, his
        grin gives way to a look of
        drunken surprise, as he looks
        down the street and hears the
        confused shouting.

        CUT TO:

C-30   MED. LONG SHOT. VILLAGE STREET

        We see the Constable and
        villagers with their guns
        and sticks. There are
        cries of

                              CRIED

                        There it is! Here it comes!

(CONTINUED)

D-30   CONTINUED

from many throats. The villagers
deploy across the street
shouting in defiance and to
keep their courage up.

CUT TO:

C-31   ANOTHER PART OF VILLAGE
STREET. MED. SHOT

The monster is coming toward
camera and the villagers.
Shouts are heard. The drink
keeps him from realizing that
they seem to attack him. He
even stretches out his arms toward them, as though in mute
appeal for companionship from
these creatures who look vaguely
like himself.

A small mongrel yellow half-starved
dog rushes up to the monster. The
monster stops. Is this another
kind of enemy? But the dog wags
its tail and jumps up and down against
him in the friendliest fashion.
The monster, starved for sympathy
and companionship, is deeply touched, he slowly reaches down his
huge hand and plays with the dog's
head.

As the monster makes friends with
the dog, there's a shout from
the crowd and a stone hits the
monster in the face.

CUT TO:

C-32   CLOSE SHOT. MONSTER

He slowly raises one hand to
his forehead, removes it,
looks at the blood. A change
from drunken good-nature to
rage comes over his face as he
glanced at his enemies. More
stones are thrown, some whizzing
past him and some falling at
his face. One or two strike
him. He turns and retreats
up the street.

CUT TO:

C-33   MED. LONG SHOT. VILLAGE ST.

Monster's back is seen as he
goes up street and behind him
we see the three villagers, two
with guns and one with a club,
who were sent around by the
Constable to cut off his retreat.
The two men with guns raise them
and fire.

CUT TO:

C-34   CLOSE SHOT. MONSTER

He is struck by a bullet.
He reels and clasps his
hand to his shoulder. His
face is now streaming with
blood from the stone. With
a bellow of rage he turns
away from his enemies who
have wounded him. But his retreat is cut off in both
directions.

CUT TO:

C-35   MED. SHOT. VILLAGE ST.

The Constable is leading his
group of villagers toward the
monster. Constable raises
his blunderbuss to fire.

CUT TO:

C-36   MED. SHOT ANOTHER PART OF ST.

Monster sees the raised gun.
He knows now that it was from
a gun that his wound came. He
looks about him like a trapped
animal. Then, with a cry, he
leaps across the narrow street
and throws himself with all
his strength against the apparently solid whitewashed wall
of a small house.

His strength is so great that
the wall crashes down and he
disappears into the hole he
has made amid broken plaster
and splintered timbers.

CUT TO:

C-37   LONG SHOT STREET

        showing all the villagers
        rushing to the wrecked house
        and shouting.

        CUT TO:

C-38   REAR OF WRECKED HOUSE
        MED. SHOT

        The monster, covered with
        plaster and dirt, climbs
        out through the wreck. The
        whole small fabric of the house
        has fallen down.

        CUT TO:

C-39   REAR OF WRECKED HOUSE.
        MED. SHOT

        The monster, covered with
        plaster and dirt, climbs
        out through the wreck. The
        whole small fabric of the house
        has fallen down.

        CUT TO:

C-39   MED. LONG SHOT REAR OF
        WRECKED HOUSE

        showing steep foothill of
        mountain with pine trees
        rising immediately behind it.
        The monster, now on all fours,
        is climbing up hill with amazing
        speed for his bulk. He is followed
        by the stray dog that made friends
        with him. The Constable and two
        or three other villagers climb
        through the debris, raise their
        guns and fire after him. But the
        monster has gained the shelter of
        some trees.

        CUT TO:

C-40   LONG SHOT MOUNTAIN GULLY

        cut off at far end by an
        apparently inaccessible cliff.
        Monster, dog behind him, is
        seen toiling up the gulley,
        pursued by villagers streaming
        past camera, shouting with joy.
        Now they have him trapped.

C-41   END OF GULLEY. FOOT OF CLIFF
        MED. SHOT

        The monster, his progress apparently
        stopped, turns and looks back.
        There are shouts from down the
        gulley.   (CONTINUED)

111

C-41   CONTINUED:

The mongrel dog has somehow
allied himself with the Monster, his
new friend, as dogs sometimes will.
He turns and barks defiance at the
villagers. The Monster looks
up at the cliff, then down at
the dog. He intends to escape,
but seems anxious not to leave
the dog.

CUT TO:

C-42   MED. SHOT LOOKING STRAIGHT
        UP CLIFF THROUGH MONSTER'S
        EYES.

It is the one way of escape,
but it seems absolutely un-
climable.

While Camera is shooting up
the cliff, a shot is heard and
a canine yelp of pain.

CUT TO:

C-43   CLOSE SHOT MONSTER

looking down, dumb surprise
at the dead dog killed at
his feet. Surprise gives
way to pain as he kneels
and feels the body. The yells
from the villagers come near.
A bullet strikes the cliff
just behind him, splintering
the stone.

CAMERA DRAWS BACK as Monster
at bay, turns, scales the
cliff like a cat and disappears
out of camera around a turn in
the rock.

CUT TO:

(NOTE: This can be worked
with concealed pegs or a
ladder. The action should
make it appear that the
monster's skill in climbing
is beyond the power of man
to emulate.)

C-44   MED. SHOT CONSTABLE AND
         VILLAGER. FOOT OF CLIFF

         standing baffled and awed,
         looking up and muttering to
         each other, dog's body lying
         at foot of cliff.

         CUT TO:

C-45   MOUNTAIN VALLEY - EXT. LOW
         HOVEL - LONG SHOT.

         Beyond this abandoned
         outhouse, partly overgrown
         by undergrowth and evidently
         long disused, a cottage is
         seen at a distance of a hundred
         feet or so. The hovel, perhaps
         one the shack of a woodcutter,
         is sheltered from direct ob-
         servation by some trees. Beyond
         the cottage, which is surrounded
         by a few stony, but cultivated
         field, is seen a towering
         mountain. The scene is one of
         the isolated little farms in
         the high foothills where lonely farm-
         ers eke out a bare existence far
         from any neighbors.

         CUT TO:

C-46   MED. LONG SHOT EXT. HOVEL

         Monster, exhausted from
         his flight and the pain
         from his wounded shoulder,
         which he holds with one
         hand, staggers out from
         behind a tree and looks
         across at the cottage.
         He does not dare show himself..

         CONTINUED:

113

C-46   CONTINUED:

        he knows now well enough what
        to expect from men. He
        turns and sees the abandoned
        hovel. Cautiously he pulls
        away the debris that blocks
        the half ruined door, pulls
        it open, peers in cautiously.
        There is only the bare floor,
        but it is shelter, and a
        place to hide. He creeps
        inside.

        CUT TO:

C-47   INT. HOVEL SHOOTING FROM DOOR
        CLOSE SHOT

        In the dim light we see the
        monster, face down on the floor
        his shoulders shaking, and we
        hear him sobbing.

        LAP DISSOLVE

DISSOLVE IN:

D-1   EXT. FIELD ... DAY ... MED. SHOT

An attractive young woman, in
native costume with a handker-
chief tied over head, is
miling a rather skinny cow.
The cow is skinny because the
field is full of stones and
yields scant pasturage.

CAMERA TRUCKS BACK showing
Monster lying behind tree
near his hovel, where he can't
be seen, watching with great
curiousity. He turns his head
and looks off in another direction as the sound of wood
chopping is heard.

CUT TO:

D-2   MED. LONG SHOT ... EDGE OF WOODS

A sturdy, handsome young peasant,
the husband of the girl with
the cow, is chopping up fallen
branches into firewood for the
house.

CUT TO:

D-3   MED. CLOSE SHOT MONSTER
       BEHIND TREE

He rises and crawls forward
on all fours so as not to
be seen, to another point
of vantage. He pops from
behind another tree.

CUT TO:

D-4   MED. LONG SHOT PEASANT'S
       COTTAGE ACROSS FIELD

Smoke is coming out of
chimney. A little girl
is playing outside the
front door. A very old
man, walking with stick
appears in doorway.

CUT TO:

D-5   MED. SHOT EXT. COTTAGE

    It is a typical peasant's
    home as is found in the
    Jura mountain valley, built
    of stones with a thatched
    roof. There is a deserted
    stable built of rough timbers
    attached to one end of house.
    The family is too poor to keep
    a horse.

    Old man is standing in door-
    way of house. The little girl,
    aged about five, drops her toy
    and runs to him holding out
    her hand.

                        CHILD
                    I'm here, Grandpa!

                OLD MAN   (stretching out left hand,
                            supporting himself with
                            stick in right hand.)
                    Come and lend me your eyes,
                    Little Hertha.

    The child puts her hand in
    the old man's and leads him
    down the steps. She guides
    him into a little walk. We
    see that he is blind.

    The young woman we saw milking
    the cow, Hilda, comes into
    scene carrying milk pail. The
    child dances up and down in
    glee, still holding old man's
    hand, saying:

                        CHILD
                    Mother's here, Grandpa!
                    Mother has the milk, and
                    here comes Daddy!

    The young peasant, Eric
    enters scene, carrying a
    bundle of firewood on his
    back, which he dumps at the
    door. He comes up and lifts
    the child in his arms and
    kisses her, then takes milk
    pail from his wife and starts
    for door.

    CUT TO:

D-6   CLOSE SHOT TREE ... MONSTER
        LYING BEHIND IT, WATCHING

DISSOLVE TO:

D-7   MED. LONG SHOT PEASANT'S HOUSE ... NIGHT

        shooting at angle towards the
        wooden stable built against the
        wall.

        Out of the shadows comes the Mon-
        ster, walking cautiously, to avoid
        observation. The one window of the
        cottage is lit from within.

        CUT TO:

D-8   EXT. STABLE ... NIGHT MED. CLOSE SHOT

        Monster comes into scene, prowls
        about, finds wooden door leading
        into outbuilding is unlatched. He
        enters it.

        CUT TO:

D-9   INT. STABLE ... NIGHT ... CLOSE SHOT

        At first it is dark, but the murmur
        of the family's voices is heard. Then
        the Monster pries out a round piece of
        wood from knot-hole, and as he does so
        the light from the living-room comes
        through hole, showing the Monster's
        face and shoulders and his hand hold-
        ing the piece of wood from the hole.
        He is lying on a sort of shelf, a
        crib orininally built to hold hay or
        corn for horse. He applies his eye
        to the knot-hole.

        CUT TO:

D-10   INT. COTTAGE ... LIVING ROOM ... FULL SHOT

        as seen by Monster through the
        knot-hole. The family of four have
        finished their evening meal. There
        is no meat, only rough peasant bread,
        vegetables dug from their little
        garden, and milk.

        The old grandfather is seated in
        a large chair, smiling benignly,
        while the father and mother are
        giving the little girl a reading
        lesson. They are down on the
        floor with the child. Before the
        child is spread an elementary first
        reader, a large book with pictures

        (CONTINUED)

D-10   CONTINUED

    of the objects described,
and their names in large
type.

    In the room is a bed, a
plaster Virgin and Child
in a niche over the bed, fire
on hearth.

    CUT TO:

D-11   CLOSE SHOT CHILD

    pointing delightedly to open
page of book. A picture of
a cow, with C O W in large
type. Pictures of milk pail
and of other things as named
by child.

> CHILD
> Cow! Milk!
> (she points to other
> pictures, naming the
> things illustrated,
> then turns the page
> and continues)
> Mother. Father. Girl.
> House. Dog. Gun. Sun-
> day. Night

    When she makes a mistake
in pronunciation as with
"hus" for "house", one of
the parents correct her,
giving her the correct
pronunciation.

> HILDA
> That's enough for tonight,
> Little Hertha. Come to Mother.
> (she picks her up)

> CHILD   (protesting)
> I don't want to go to bed.

    She stretches out her arms
to her father, who says:

> ERIC
> Be good girl. Daddy will
> come in and say goodnight.

> HILDA
> A goodnight kiss for Grandpa.

    (CONTINUED)

118

D-11   CONTINUED

She carries the child over
and the child leans out of
her mother's arms and kisses
the old man, who strokes her
head.

> GRANDFATHER
> Sweet dreams, and tomorrow
> I'll borrow your eyes again.

As mother carries child out
of rooom, the old man gropes
on table. Eric springs to
his side.

> ERIC
> Here, Father!

Eric picks up a fiddle
just out of the Old Man's
reach and hands it to him.
The Old Man begins to play
a tender, old-fashioned
melody. He plays beauti-
fully. Eric sits watching
him in rapt silence.

CUT TO:

D-12   CLOSEUP MONSTER'S FACE

We can see his face clearly
in the light streaming through
the knot-hole. Powerfully
affected by the music, there
are tears streaming down the
uncouth visage.

DISSOLVE TO:

D-13   INT. MONSTER'S HOVEL
        DAY ... CLOSE SHOT

The Monster is stretched
out on his stomach, facing
entrance of hovel, which he
has partly blocked with boughs
and leaves, but enough light
comes through for him to be
able to study the child's book,
which he has stolen. He is
repeating the words as he heard
the child and its parents pro-
nounce them, and as he does
so he puts his finger on the
thing described.

CUT TO:

119

D-14   CLOSEUP BOOK

looking down over Monster's
shoulder. We see pictures of
a cow, buckets of milk, a father,
a mother, and child, a house,
with the words spelled out beside them. This should be an
ordinary child's first reader,
rather large, and not too shiny
or expensive looking - the sort of
paper book, worn and torn, that
peasants would be apt to own.

                    MONSTER
                         (his finger pointing to
                         the objects as he repeats
                         the words)
                    Cow. Milk. Father. Mother.
                    Girl. House. Dog. Gun. Sun.
                    Day. Night.

DISSOLVE TO:

D-15   MED. CLOSE SHOT ... FIELD
         NIGHT

On the rocky soil the peasants
have planted vegetables -
cabbages and turnips. The
Monster is seen rooting some
of these out and munching them.

CUT TO:

D-16   ANOTHER PART OF FIELD ... NIGHT
         MED. SHOT

The family cow is lying asleep.
Monster approaches, carrying a
pail he has stolen. He grunts
at cow, shakes it by the horns,
to make her get up. Finally he
kicks her.

                    MONSTER
                         (practising his first
                         words)
                    Cow! Milk!

Cow rises. Monster carefully
places pail under cow's teats
and starts trying to milk her.
His lack of skill annoys the
cow, which is restive, but he
finally gets some milk. He
pulls the pail out, raises it
to his lips and drinks.

LAP DISSOLVE TO:

D-17   WOODS ... WINTER ... MOONLIGHT
           MED. SHOT

           This scene must be distinctly
           wintery as we use it to show
           lapse of some months. Where
           before we saw autumnal scene
           with leaves still on trees,
           there is a foot of snow on the
           ground now. Snow lies heavily
           on the trees.

           The Monster is splitting up some
           wood with Eric's ax. He has al-
           ready split up a considerable
           amount. Now he gathers up the
           wood in his arms.

           CUT TO:

D-18   EXT. PEASANT'S COTTAGE ...WINTER
           MOONLIGHT ... MED. SHOT

           Monster carries his armful of
           wood down path, which has been
           carefully shovelled clear of
           snow so that he leaves no foot-
           steps. He lowers the wood
           quietly in front of the door
           and retires silently.

           The pile of wood left by the
           Monster during the night is
           outside door. The door opens
           and little Hertha peeps out.
           She claps her hands delightedly
           and calls within.

                          HERTHA
                  Mother! Daddy! The good
                  fairy's been here again!

           She dances about in glee
            as her Father and Mother
           come out. The child points
           to the pile of wood.

           Eric and Hilda look at the
           wood, then turn to each
           other with awe and wonder,
           ignoring the child.

           (CONTINUED)

                HILDA   (in low tones to her
                                  husband
            Again! Who can have done this?

Eric shakes his head in
dumb wonderment. His
wife shows that she considers
this some supernatural dispen-
sation by turning to Eric
with shining eyes and crossing
herself. Eric shakes his head
again. He can find no words
to express his wonder. They
turn back into the house.

DISSOLVE TO:

D-20   STABLE ADJOINING COTTAGE ... NIGHT

The screen is in complete
darkness. The wooden stopper
in the knot-hole is removed
by Monster's hand as before,
and we see him by the light
streaming in through knot-hole
lying on wooden shelf. He
applies eye to knot-hole
shutting off light as we

CUT TO:

D-21   INT COTTAGE ... NIGHT
FULL SHOT

as seen by Monster through
knot-hole. It is near the
family bedtime. The child
is already asleep in the next
room, the Old Grandfather is
just finishing a last selec-
tion on his fiddle. Eric
and Hilda are sitting on the
floor listening in rapt
attention, hand in hand.

It is winter now and cold -
there is a warm fire burning
in the open hearth. The
Grandfather's chair has been
moved before the fire and his
son and daughter-in-law crouch
before him near the fire.
A single taper burns on the
table.

(CONTINUED)

The Old Man lays down the
fiddle, there is a moment's
silence. Then he rises,

                    OLD MAN
            Good night, my children.

He stretches out his arms.
They both rise and go to
him. With his hand he feels
the wife's face and kisses
her brow. He reaches for
his son's hand and shakes it.
He turns and feels his way
towards door of his little
bedroom, his son helping him.
Then the husband and wife turn
back to the center table. Beyond it is a crude bed where
they sleep. Above head of
bed, in a little niche, stands
a plaster Virgin holding the
Infant Christ. The two stand
for a moment, his arm lovingly
around her shoulders.

                    HILDA
            Eric, I wish you'd heard
            Little Hertha reading to
            Brandpa before you came in -
            she understands everything -
            she's learned to read as well
            as I can in these few months...

Eric picks up book from
table that is bound in
black oilcloth, so that we'll
recognize it again.

                    ERIC
            A child that age - reading this!
            It would be tough for most
            children of eight or ten.
                    (he puts book down)

                    HILDA
            When she reads to him Grandpa
            explains all the hard words -
            so a child's mind can take
            it all in.

            ERIC   (He shakes his head again)
            That wood, Hilda! The nearest
            neighbor is three miles off,
            and Old Hogan would never do a
            thing like that!

                    HILDA
            There's some good influence
            Eric, watching over us. I can
            feel it.

D-21   (CT'D) - 2

Hilda and Eric are now ready
for bed. She steps over to the
bed, then looks around and
motions to Eric with her right
hand to join her. He comes up and
takes her hand and they bow
together on their knees for
a goodnight prayer before the
statue of the Virgin and Child.
The little byplay shows that she
is a devout Believer, and he
joins her in prayer to please her.

CUT TO:

D-22   CLOSE SHOT MONSTER'S FACE

Peering through knothole.
The light is on his face.
It suddenly diminishes.. now
we see his face very faintly.

CUT TO:

D-23   INT. COTTAGE ROOM. MED.
        CLOSE SHOT

The taper on table has been
extinguished, the fire has
died down. Eric is seated
on the bed taking down his wife's
long hair, which flows over her
shoulders, as he mutters of
love, and kisses her hands.

                    ERIC   (Mumbling)
                         Hilda, if only I weren't a
                         poor man.. If only I could
                         give you what women have
                         in the towns..where there ain't
                         a woman worth your little finger.

                    HILDA   (she puts her hand over
                                 his mouth with a little
                                 rippling laugh of love.
                         When you gave me yourself,
                         and then little Hertha, you
                         gave me all I needed to make
                         me the happiest woman in
                         the Juras.

She puts her arms around
his neck and he crushes her
mouth against his as she falls
back on the bed.

CUT TO:

D-24   INT. OUTBUILDING - CLOSEUP
        MONSTER'S HEAD AT KNOTHOLE

        We see tears again pouring
        down his cheeks as he draws
        sharp sighs.

        DISSOLVE TO:

D-25   CLOSE SHOT MONSTER'S
        HOVEL - DAY

        This time we see snow on
        the bushes that block the
        entrance. He is wrapped
        in his coat. He is studying
        a book as before, lying on
        his stomach. But this time
        it isn't the child's first
        reader, but the volume bound
        in black oilcloth that we saw
        last. Again he is pronouncing
        the words as read by the child
        to her grandfather and explained
        by him to her. He stumbles a
        little, but we see that during
        these months he has taught
        himself by constant eavesdropping
        to read simple words, and, in
        reading them, to speak them.

        What he reads is a simple little
        love passage, suitable for a child,
        and yet poignant to him, who has
        learned about the love of man for
        woman, and human companionship,
        during his long vigils at the
        knothole.

        Monster reads with difficulty,
        pronouncing every syllable, in
        words of more than one syllable,
        as that it were a separate word.

                        MONSTER   (reading)
                    "And she kissed the brave knight
                    and said: 'I will be your only
                    true love', and so they were mar-
                    ried and lived happ-il-y ever after."

        Monster closes book, and pulls
        out from an inner pocket of his
        hacket - the same garment he
        has worn through both pictures -
        a tattered note book. He opens
        this.

        CUT TO:

D-26   CLOSEUP NOTE BOOK

        CAMERA SHOOTING OVER Monster's
        shoulder. We read:

        (CONTINUED)

D-27   INSERT.

"University of Goldstadt.
Notes by Henry Frankenstein."

Description in detail of experiments resulting in my
creation of a living sub-man
from dead human tissue."

CUT TO:

D-28   CLOSE SHOT MONSTER

Trying to puzzle this out.
The words are too long. He
has heard nothing of this sort
from the simple peasants, and
he shakes his head and gives
it up. He carefully folds the
note book and puts it back in
his pocket, and turns again to
the little girl's book.

LAP DISSOLVE TO:

D-29   MED. LONG SHOT PINE WOODS..
         DAY.. SPRING

         (No more snow, the flowers and
         leaves are out again; so the
         monster has had more time to
         learn.)

         A young rustic, carrying hunting
         rifle, is walking, arm-in-arm
         with a peasant girl. They are
         talking in low tones. We don't
         hear what they say. Suddenly
         the rustic drops his gun, grabs
         the girl in his arms and kisses her.
         She pulls back and slaps him
         in the face. Then, with a peal of
         laughter, she jumps behind a tree
         and is gone. We hear her laugh come
         from the woods. The rustic accepts the
         challenge, picks up his gun and
         with a threatening shout, starts chase.

                                RUSTIC
                         I'll find you.. you can't
                         hide from me!

         He plunges after her.
         CUT TO:

D-30   BANK OF SWIFT STREAM.. MED. SHOT

         The girl, continuing her game
         of hide-and-seek, still laughing
         runs along the bank of the stream.

         Just before her th euncouth
         form of the monster rises out
         of some bushes. She sees him, gives
         a scream of surprise and terror, her
         foot slips and she falls over the
         bank into the stream. The monster
         rushes out to edge of bank and
         looks down.

         BUT TO:

D-31   MED. CLOSE SHOT STREAM..
         SHOOTING FROM BANK

         The girl can't swim.. she's
         struggling in the current and
         is carried beyond her depth.

         CUT TO:

D-32   MED. SHOT MONSTER ON BANK

Girl in stream. Monster leaps
down into water, which because of
his great height isn't out of
his depth. He wades out to girl
where the water is up to his neck
grabs her under one arm, wades
back and clambers up the bank,
drapping his burden with him. He lays
the unconscious girl on ground
and, with solicitude and anxiety
in his face, he kneels beside her.
He is anxious to help, but he
doesn't know what to do. His hands
flutter over her. A cry of horror
and rage comes over sound track
from peasant. The monster looks
up and rises.

CUT TO:

D-33   MED. LONG SHOT FOREST

Peasant is raising his rifle.
He fires.

CUT TO:

D-34   CLOSE SHOT MONSTER

The bullet strikes his arm.
He tries to raise it. The
bone is broken. Snarling
with pain and rage he turns
and with bent head and shoulders
bounds out of scene.

The young peasant, who has
dropped his rifle, runs into
scene. He throws himself beside
the girl, and begins pumping her
arms. In a few seconds she
revives and throws her arms
around his neck.

DISSOLVE TO:

D-35   MED. SHOT FIELD.. SPRING.. DAY

Eric, strapped to one of the
primitive wooden plows still
used in that region, is pulling
plow through the poor soil. A
few furrows have already been
turned. His wife is guiding the
plow. Behind her trips little
Hertha, having a lovely time
dropping three or four kernels every
two feet and covering them up with
her fingers.

CUT TO:

D-36   CLOSE SHOT TREE** NEAR MONSTER'S
       HOVEL

He is looking off, evidently
watching the family at the
plow. Now the moment he has been
planning for has come. The
husband, mother and child he is
afraid to face. He knows the effect
he has on everybody. But in his
crying need for companionship, kindness
and love he has decided to appeal to
the old man, who can't see him.
Perhaps the old man will intercede
for him with the others. He starts
to move off sideways, keeping
the trees so that the family in
the field can't see him.

CUT TO:

D-37   EXT. COTTAGE.. DAY..MED. SHOT

The monster approaches the door.
He's come around by an angle so
that he can't be seen from the
field. His knees shake under
him from apprehension and shyness.
He has spent nearly a year spying
on these people, learning to talk,
learning about their life, and
now he puts his fate to the test.

He raises his right hand to knock.
We notice that his left arm,
where he was shot while trying
to rescue the drowning girl, hangs
limp. It has not fully recovered. After
registering shyness and fear again,
he raises his hand again to knock.

CUT TO:

D-38   INT. COTTAGE. DAY. MED. SHOT

The room is flooded with sun-
light from the one window. There
is a fire burning on the hearth.
The Old Grandfather, his fiddle
on his knee, sits in his armchair
day-dreaming. He lifts his head
as he hears a gentle knock at the
outer door. He shows surprise
that a visitor should come to
this lonely cottage. He calls:

                    OLD MAN
                         Come in!

CAMERA PANS to door. It
opens cautiously. The Monster stands there, tongue-
tied and embarrassed, his
face working convulsively.
His youth is too dry to start
practicing these human sounds
he has so long practiced by
himself.

                    OLD MAN
                              (gentle and calm and
                              courteous at all time)

                    Yes?

Monster's tongue still
cleaves to the roof of his
mouth and he trembles all
over. The Blind Man has
heard the door open and
thinks this silence strange.
The most natural explanation
would be a weary traveller anxious
for food and drink and unwilling
to ask for it. So the Blind
Man tries to help him out.

                    OLD MAN

                         If you've come to ask for food
                         or drink you're welcome to what
                         little we have. But you must
                         find it yourself. I can't see...
                         These old eyes.....

                    MONSTER
                         I know you can not see me. That
                         is why I came.

This is a strange remark,
still more the Monster's
strange gutteral accent,
astonishes the old man.

                    OLD MAN
                         I don't understand. Who
                         are you?

(CONTINUED)

                              130

                    MONSTER

                        I do not know.

              OLD MAN

                        You do not wish to tell me?
                        A smuggler, perhaps?

                    MONSTER

                        If your eyes could see, you
                        would hate me. You would get
                        gun - or stone - or fire -

              OLD MAN

                        Why should I hate you, my friend?

                    MONSTER

                        All men hate me.

              OLD MAN

                        Hadn't you better tell me who
                        you are? And where you come
                        from?

                    MONSTER

                        I do not know.

              OLD MAN
                        The blind are sensitive to voices
                        because they can't see faces,
                        and I can tell that you are
                        unhappy, and that you mean no
                        harm. Won't you be frank with
                        me? Come, who are you?
                            (Monster shakes head, dumbly)
                        You say all men hate you - have
                        you committed some crime?

The Monster is not capable
of carrying on a conversation
and he can't explain himself
since he doesn't yet know what
or who he is. He shakes his
head again, dumbly.

                    MONSTER

                        Make sound for me with that
                        box. It makes me sad, but it
                        makes me happy.

              OLD MAN
                            (startled, puts his hand
                             on fiddle)
                        But I play only here, to my
                        children. You can't have heard
                        me.....

(CONTINUED)

                    MONSTER
                              (interrupting eagerly)
                    Each night, I hear you.

                    OLD MAN
                              (incredulous)
                    Each night! But if you hear
                    me play, where are you?

                    MONSTER

                    Each night I lie in there -
                    I see through hole in wood. I
                    watch - I learn.

                    OLD MAN
                              (astonished)
                    In there? In the old stable?
                    Then it was you who cut the
                    wood, who brought us game
                    from the forest! But why?

                    MONSTER

                    All men hate me. I want friends
                    - I want love -

                    OLD MAN

                    Then you've lived alone, here
                    in the woods - have you no
                    family - no friends?

                    MONSTER

                    No.

Now over come by emotion,
he flings himself at the
Old Man's feet. Even on
his knees his head seems
to come up to the Old Man's.
He half sobs as he begs and
pleads.

                    MONSTER

                    No friends - no mate - no love -
                    no father - no mother - you
                    my friends, my only friends.
                    Let me live here. Let me work
                    for you - I am strong...

The Old Man is powerfully
moved by the visitor's
distress and evident
sincerity.

                    OLD MAN

                    I will speak to my children -
                    we will do what we can for you.

(CONTINUED)

132

D-38   (CONTINUED -3)

The Monster starts to sob
inarticulately in gratitude.

CUT TO:

D-39   TWO SHOT MONSTER KNEELING
        BEFORE OLD MAN.

favoring old Man. As he
speaks, the Old Man gropes
with his right hand and
places it on the Monster's
head, soothingly. A startled
expression comes into his
face as he feels the vast
cranium. Not horror, but in-
credulous astonishment. He
passes his hand down the Monster's neck and across his
huge shoulder.

CUT TO:

D-40   INT. COTTAGE. CLOSE SHOT
        OUTER DOOR.

It opens and Little Hertha
trips in, stops, her mouth
open. She gives a scream of
terror, then runs out leaving
the door open.

CUT TO:

D-51   MED. CLOSE SHOT OLD MAN
        IN CHAIR. MONSTER KNEELING
        BEFORE HIM.

The Old Man, horrified at
the child's scream, rises to
his feet. The Monster raises
his great bulk from the floor,

                    OLD MAN
                 What is it?
                      (appeals to Monster)
                 That was Little Hertha - some-
                 thing has terrified her - go and
                 see, my friend.

The Monster slowly turns toward
the door, his face working
convulsively.

CUT TO:

133

D-42   INT. COTTAGE MED. SHOT. DOOR

        Eric bursts in, carrying ax,
        the ax the Monster used to
        cut the family's wood - behind
        him appears Hilda. Hilda screams
        with terror.

        BUT TO:

D-43   FULL SHOT ROOM - TAKING IN
        MONSTER AND OLD MAN

        The Monster puts one arm
        around the Old Man's shoulders,
        in a vague appeal to him for
        protection and explanation.
        Eric, ready anyway to do battle
        with this hideous apparition,
        interprets Monster's gesture
        as an attack on his father.
        He shouts to his wife.

                        ERIC
                  Get Father out!

        He advances on Monster,
        the ax raised to strike.
        Monster bounds around table
        putting table between himself
        and Eric. As he does so he
        gives his old guttural growl
        of rage and menace. Hilda
        seizes the Old Man's hand and
        drags him to the door, scream-
        ing back over her shoulder.

                        HILDA
                        (screaming)
                  It's coming straight from hell,
                  Eric, it'll kill you! It's a
                  devil!

        CUT TO:

D-44   CLOSE SHOT MONSTER & ERIC.

        The table between them. Eric
        aims murderous blow with the
        ax across the table at the Mon-
        ster's head. The Monster dodges
        and the ax wounds his shoulder
        only slightly, falling to the
        floor. The Monster now starts
        to pursue Eric around the table
        but Eric keeps the table between
        them. Monster clambers on table.

        CUT TO:

D-45   CLOSE SHOT MONSTER

        standing on table. This
        makes him look twice as big
        as ever. He foams with rage
        and crouches to spring on Eric.

        CUT TO:

D-46   FULL SHOT ROOM.

        Eric disappears through door as
        the Monster springs to floor. The
        Monster is now berserk with fury.
        He picks up ax and rushes to door,
        then he turns and begins to swing
        az violently, smashing the furniture.
        He swings. He smashes the plaster Virgin and
        Child in niche. He picks up the
        Old Man's fiddle and dashes it to
        pieces on floor. He wrecks chairs
        and the table. He pulls out the
        crude bed, rips it to pieces, then
        begins hurling the pieces of bed,
        table and chairs into the fire.

        CUT TO:

D-47   LONG SHOT AS SEEN FROM COTTAGE

        Across the field we see the ter-
        rified family fleeing, the Mother
        carrying the little girl, Eric
        leading the Old Blind Man, who
        stumbles along at a half-run as
        fast as his old legs will carry
        him.

        CUT TO:

D-48   INT. ROOM. FULL SHOT.

        The Monster stands at end of
        room nearest door, still panting
        with rage and misery, rears now
        running down his cheek. The other
        end of the room is a roaring furn-
        ace, for the fire in the hearth has
        caught hold on the wrecked furniture
        that the Monster tossed into it and
        around it.

        CUT TO:

D-49   EXT. STOCK SHOT. NIGHT

        The burning cottage is now seen
        a mass of flames.

        DISSOLVE TO:

E-1   MOUNTAIN VALLEY - DAY
        MED. LONG SHOT - DESERTED PATH

        A middle-aged man, in black
        coat, carrying a bundle
        of books tied together with
        straps, looking like the
        village school master, is
        coming along path.

        As he approaches the camera
        the monster rises from
        behind large boulder.

        Seeing the creature before
        him, the school-master
        throws his bundle of books
        away and stares with open
        mouth, his knees shaking under
        him. He turns to flee, but
        in one bound the monster is
        on him. He puts his hands
        on his shoulders and forces
        him to his knees. The school-
        master is gibbering with
        terror. The monster steps
        back and pulls out Henry's
        Frankenstein's note book from
        inside pocket of old coat
        that he has worn through
        both pictures. It is stained
        and tattered. He throws book
        down at feel of kneeling school-
        master. He points to it and
        peremptorily orders:

                        MONSTER

                    Read!

        But the school-master is
        too paralyzed with fright
        to pick up the book, or do
        anything but gibber.

        Monster drops on one knee
        grabs school-master's throat
        and chokes him, a sufficient
        warning of his fate if he
        disobeys orders. Monster
        rises and repeats his gesture
        to note book and his order.

                        MONSTER
                        Read!

        With shaking hands, the
        schoolmaster picks up note
        book and opens it.

        CUT TO:

                            136

E-2   INSERT:

Henry Frankenstein's open
note book, held in the
schoolmaster's shaking hands
We read"

          "University of Goldstadt.
          Notes by Henry Frankenstein.

          Description in detail of ex-
          periments resulting in my
          creation of a living sub-man
          from dead human tissue."

As the insert is held Schoolmaster's
shaking voice reading the above
lines comes over the sound track.
His hand turns a page as we

DISSOLVE OUT:

DISSOLVE IN:

E-3   CLOSE SHOT SCHOOLMASTER

reading as before. As he
comes to the end of the
notes the Monster is standing motionless, his head
bent forward, listening
intently.

                    SCHOOLMASTER
                        (reading)
                "This record is for my eyes alone.
                No future scientist must be tempted
                to repeat my ominous and disast-
                rous work. One horrible task re-
                mains. This foul creature must
                never leave the dark room where I
                keep him imprisoned. Murder? Is
                it murder to kill a thing in man's
                image who is not a man? A creature
                without a soul? And this thing I
                have made is lower than a beast.
                I must do it. I shall place these
                notes in the jacket that the monster
                wears and bury them with his corpse
                then return to Elizabeth and my
                family in Belrive and try to forget
                my crimes. May God forgive me!
                Henry Frankenstein."

The schoolmaster drops the
note book on ground and
looks up at the monster.

CONTINUED:

The monster has forgotten
him. Now, for the first
time, he knows who and what
his is, why he had no child-
hood, no parents, why he must
forever be an outcast.

In a voice charged with hate and
desire for vengeance he says
looking out:

                    MONSTER

          Hen-ry Frank-en-stein!
          Bel-rive!

He lowers his head, looks
at the crouching schoolmaster,
and with one shove from his
powerful boot knocks him
across path, where school
master lies moaning. The
monster picks up the note
book, puts it in his
pocket and turns out of
scene.

SEQUENCE "F"

F-1   INT. CASTLE FRANKENSTEIN
        MED SHOT DRAWINGROOM

        Elizabeth is talking to
        Father Gerard. He sits
        with his Priest's hat on his
        knee opposite her. Elizabeth
        is now the Baroness Frankenstein,
        the bride of Henry, who has suc-
        ceeded to his murdered father's
        title.

                        FATHER GERARD
                            My dear Baroness, we all know
                            who's responsible for the
                            change in Henry since you
                            marriage.

                        ELIZABETH   (with a laugh)
                            It was your marriage, Father.
                            You kept at him until there
                            was nothing else for poor Henry
                            to do but marry me.

                        FATHER GERARD   (smiling)
                            Yes, he's the first man I ever
                            knew who didn't want to marry
                            a woman because he loved her
                            so much.

                        ELIZABETH (now serious)
                            I know.

                        FATHER GERARD   (serious)
                            And you were the only cure for
                            his obsession of guilt - the
                            strange delusion that he some-
                            how manufactured that murderous
                            lunatic out of corpses, and
                            brought him to life.

                        ELIZABETH (She knows the truth and
                                    she's not anxious to con-
                                    tinue this topic)
                            Oh, that's all over. The mad-
                            man, or whoever he was, hasn't
                            been heard of in a year. He
                            must have perished of cold or
                            hunger...

                        (CONTINUED)

                          FATHER GERARD   (a little uneasily)
                               I'm not so sure. A madman
                               burned a peasant's cottage
                               in the mountain valley above
                               Ingolstadt not long ago - and
                               the description might fit the
                               monster who murdered Henry's
                               poor father.

Elizabeth rises, white-
faced, trying to keep her
composure.

                     ELIZABETH
                          Father, not a word of this to
                          Henry, please. If he heard it,
                          it might bring back those -
                          fancies he had when he was so
                          ill. Even yet, he has dreams -
                          dreadful dreams -

                     FATHER GERARD   (also rising)
                          Of course not, my dear Baroness,
                          But he may hear of it. If this
                          man is at large there may be
                          other - incidents. And I
                          thought I must warn you.

They turn as they hear
a noise.

F-2   MED CLOSE SHOT DOOR
       OF LIVINGROOM

Henry comes in. He has
changed greatly, since we
last saw him. His married
happiness, his belief because
of the long absence of any
news that the Monster must
have perished, have made a
new man of him. He calls
cheerily..
                     HENRY
                          Ah, Father Gerard! You old
                          matchmaker!

He goes over and throws
his arm around his wife,
and kisses her. Father
Gerard comes up with out-
stretched hand to say goodbye.
                          Oh, don't go! I've seen noth-
                          ing of you...

                     FATHER GERARD   (smiling)
                          Your poor old priest is the
                          only busy man in Frankenstein.
                          Two christenings today.

                     HENRY
                          Well, if you really must keep
                          in practice...maybe some day
                          Elizabeth and I will have one
                          of those jobs for you.
                                   (CONTINUED)

F-2   CONTINUED

        Henry laughs and shakes
        hands with him. Priest
        turns to say goodbye to
        Elizabeth.

F-3   EXT. HALL. CASTLE FRANKENSTEIN
        CLOSE SHOT EDWARD & JUSTINE

        Justine is showing Edward a
        miniature of Elizabeth, in an
        old gold frame, with a chain
        so that she can wear it around
        her neck.

                              EDWARD   (in awe)
                                    Gold! That's worth more money
                                    than you ever saw, Justine.

                              JUSTINE   (indignantly)
                                    You think I'd sell for money
                                    the picture of herself the
                                    Baroness gave me because I
                                    helped her nurse poor Master
                                    Henry...?
                              EDWARD
                                    Didn't say you would.

                              JUSTINE   (looks up at him archly)
                                    The same place tonight?
                              EDWARD
                                    I've the harness to clean
                                    after supper - may be a little
                                    late.
                              JUSTINE
                                    Mind you don't keep me waiting-
                                    it's lonely in those woods.

        Justine embraces him. As
        she is about to kiss him he
        pushes her away roughly. When
        he does this her face, which
        Camera favors, shows surprise
        and anger, but he is looking
        beyond her sheepishly. Father
        Gerard's voice come over as CAMERA
        PULLS BACK showing Father Gerard
        closing door on his way out from
        drawingroom. He shakes his finger
        at them admonishingly. We see that
        he is really amused but is trying
        to be severe.

                              FATHER GERARD
                                    What's this, what's this? Why
                                    haven't you been to see me,
                                    Edward? Careful, careful.
                                    Young blood - hot blood. It's
                                    about time I posted the bans
                                    for you two, that's plain.

        Edward and Justine stand
        embarrassed during this,
        their eyes on the floor.
        DISSOLVE TO:

F-4   MED. SHOT CROSSROADS
        TWILIGHT

        An old woman with a full
        market basket is trudging
        along, a shawl over her
        head. The Monster comes
        into scene, she screams,
        drops basket, turns to flee,
        but he bounds after her and
        catches her by the arm. He
        shakes her. She drops to her
        knees, moaning, her hands out-
        stretched to him in an attitude
        of prayer.

                              OLD WOMAN
                                    Please - please, devil!
                                    Don't kill me, good, kind
                                    devil...

                              MONSTER   (in peremtory tones
                                    Bel-rive! Where Bel-rive?

        The old woman shakily
        points with her hand in
        direction of one of the
        two roads. The Monster
        turns on his heel and walks
        out of scene.
        DISSOLVE TO:

F-5   MED SHOT WOODS NEAR VILLAGE
        OF FRANKENSTEIN..MOONLIGHT

        Justine is seen walking along
        path on her way to keep her
        tryst with Edward. As she
        approaches CAMERA the Monster
        rises out of underbrush and
        confronts her. Justine screams
        and turns to flee, but with a
        leap the Monster catches her
        and swings her around to face
        him.

                              MONSTER
                                    Bel-rive! Where? Henry
                                    Frank-en-stein! Where?

        This shows us that the
        Monster is merely again
        trying to get directions,
        as from the old woman. But
        the girl doesn't understand.
        His appearance drives her out
        of her mind with terror. She
        drops to her knees, tears
        brooch of Elizabeth from her
        throat. Holds it out to him.
                              JUSTINE   (babbling)
                                    Don't kill me - take this -
                                    it's all I have - it's gold -
                                    pure gold - -   (CONTINUED)

142

F-5   CONTINUED

The Monster, puzzled, stretches out huge paw, takes brooch
and looks at it. Justine babbles on..

                    JUSTINE
                Really it's gold - Baroness
                Frankenstein told me so - it's
                her picture!

                MONSTER   (fiercely questioning)
                Frank-en-stein?

                JUSTINE   (incoherently)
                My mistress - Baron Henry
                Frankenstein's wife! - Oh
                please let me go - it's gold
                real gold - -

F-6   CLOSEUP MONSTER

looking at miniature of
Elizabeth. He can dimly see
the portrait of the beautiful
woman in the moonlight. While
the terrified girl sobs at his
feet, he mutters with all possible rage, bitterness, self-
pity.

                    MONSTER
                Wife! Mate! Love!

He draws in his breath
in a deep animal-like
half-rattle, half-hiss
of menace.

F-7   MED CLOSE MONSTER &
       JUSTINE

While the Monster brooks
on the happiness of Henry,
and his own fate as a hunted
outcast, and his projects for
vengeance on his creator, Justine thinks she sees her chance
to escape. She scrambles to her
feet and is off in the underbrush.

Something snaps in the Monster's
brain. Blind, murderous fury is
induced by his wrongs, and by his
learning that Henry, whom he knows
responsible for his woes, has a
mate when he has none. He leaps
with a cry of rage after Justine.

F-8   FLASH SHOT MONSTER

        strangling Justine.

        DISSOLVE TO:

F-9   MED CLOSE WOODS NEAR VILLAGE
        MOONLIGHT

        Edward is waiting by a big
        tree for Justine. We see that
        she is late, for he walks up
        and down impatiently, whistling.
        Finally he calls..

                              EDWARD
                         Justine! Justine!

F-10   ANOTHER PART OF WOODS..NIGHT
        MED SHOT

        It is darker, there is now no
        moon. Edward, now greatly worried,
        is hunting for the girl. He puts
        his hands to his lips and calls,
        loudly..

                              EDWARD
                         Justine! Justine! Where are
                         you?

F-11   ANOTHER PART WOODS..
        JUST BEFORE DAWN..MED SHOT

        As the first flush of morning
        creeps over the woods, Edward,
        exhausted from his long search,
        stumbles into CAMERA. Either
        he's lost his way, or is too tired
        to go further. He sits with a sigh
        on the bank to rest himself. He is
        too exhausted to keep awake, and
        flops over on his side, asleep.
        Monster enters scene. He sees the
        sleeping Edward. He comes to him,
        looks down at him as if undecided.
        He unclasps his hand and looks from
        it to the sleeping youth.

F-12   CLOSE SHOT EDWARD & MONSTER

        Monster as Justine's brooch
        of Elizabeth in his hand. He
        stoops down, slips it in Edward's
        breast pocket without wakening
        him, straightens up and turns off
        into the woods.

F-13   ANOTHER PART OF WOODS
        EARLY MORNING..MED SHOT

        Four villagers, one of them
        carrying a lantern, indicating
        that they have been searching
        thru the darkness, are beating
        thru the woods. They walk in
        extended order to cover as much
        ground as possible. The man fur-
        thest from CAMERA half stumbles
        over something and gives a cry
        of horror. The other three turn
        and hasten to him.

F-14   MED SHOT GROUP OF FOUR MEN
        AROUND JUSTINE'S BODY

        One of them is on his knees,
        examining the dead girl. He
        looks up and says..

                         VILLAGER
                    Strangled!

                    2ND VILLAGER
                    I will go to the village for
                    the Herr Burgomeister.

                    3RD VILLAGER   (grimly)
                    Aye, and for more men. 'Tis
                    that boy who was with her we
                    must be finding now!

F-14   ANOTHER PART WOODS..DAY
        MED SHOT

        The scene is beside the
        bank where the exhausted
        Edward fell asleep during
        his search. Edward is stand-
        ing, still half asleep, and
        completely confused.

        The Burgomeister and half a
        dozen fiercely suspicious vil-
        lagers are cross-examining him,

                         BURGOMEISTER
                    Where did you leave Justine
                    last night?

                    EDWARD
                         she was to meet me. She wasn't
                         there - I couldn't find her -
                         I hunted for hours - I must have
                         fallen asleep!

                         (CONTINUED)

145

F-15   CONTINUED

While Edward is talking
one of the villagers sees
the gold chain of Justine's
brooch dangling from Edward's
breast pocket. He pulls it out
and turns to the Burgomeister.
Thru what follows Edward, who
doesn't know the girl is dead
looks on in open-mouthed stupor.
Burgomeister thakes brooch. He
recognizes the miniature.

                    BURGOMEISTER
               The Baroness Frankenstein!

                    VILLAGER (to Burgomeister)
               It was Justine's - the Baroness
               gave it to her - Justine showed
               it to all of us at church.

That's enough for the
Burgomeister. He turns
fiercely on Edward and
gives and order.

                    BURGOMEISTER
               Tie his arms!

One of the peasants
whips a belt off and in
a moment is tying Edward's
arms behind his back. Edward
is still dazed.

(NOTE: I put in these next
five shots because we already
have a village and villagers in
Sequence "C", so they should
cost hardly anything. Of course
this lynching is of very subordin-
ate importance in the story, and
we don't want to make a big spec-
tacle of it, or carry it on for
any considerable footage.)

F-16   VILLAGE STREET..VILLAGE OF
        FRANKENSTEIN..LONG SHOT...DAY

Crowds of villagers in groups
are discussing the murder of
Justine. The street is buzzing
like a beehive.

F-17   GROUP OF ANGRY VILLAGERS
        MED SHOT...DAY

Men and women are surrounding
one of the men who found the
body and captured Edward.
Amid black looks and angry
cries he is giving them the
story. A few fragments of his
narrative come over sound track.   (CONTINUED)

                              VILLAGER
                         Strangled her with his bare
                         hands...tried to escape with
                         the gold brooch in his pocket
                         and fell asleep...didn't say
                         a word when I pulled the brooch
                         out of his pocket. Just stared
                         at us.

     This is interrupted by
     villagers in the group
     looking off and yelling..

                              VILLAGERS
                         Here he comes! Kill him!

     Members of group hurry
     out of CAMERA.

F-18   MED LONG SHOT VILLAGE ST.
        DAY

        Edward is standing in the
        grasp of two guards. The
        Burgomeister, before him,
        is expostulating with the
        crowd, trying to protect
        his prisoner. Father Gerard
        is seen with the Burgomeister,
        also pleading with the maddened
        villagers. But the crowd is
        closing in, shaking sticks
        and working itself up into a
        lynching mood.

F-19   EXT VILLAGE..NIGHT..MED SHOT

        Edward's body is hanging from
        branch of tree, swaying gently.

F-20   INT ELIZABETH'S BEDROOM
        MED SHOT CASTLE FRANKENSTEIN
        NIGHT

        Elizabeth, in negligee, is ly-
        ing in a state of collapse on
        a couch. Henry, his nerves
        frazzled as in the old days,
        is walking up and down biting
        his fingernails.

                              ELIZABETH (crying)
                         I keep thinking how it was my
                         little present to poor Justine-
                         because she nursed you so faith-
                         fully - but for that brooch
                         she'd never have been murdered.
                                        (CONTINUED)

                    HENRY   (looking at her, darkly)
                         I'm not so sure about that!

                    ELIZABETH
                         Edward didn't do it, and now
                         they've killed him! He was
                         no thief! I've watched their
                         little romance - he loved her
                         Henry. Why didn't they come
                         and ask us before they killed
                         him?

                    HENRY
                         The found your brooch on the
                         boy - if he didn't take it,
                         if he's innocent, what fiendish
                         malace, what devilish cunning...

        Henry stops his pacing
        and looks at her. She looks
        up at him, then drops her
F-21   CLOSE SHOT ELIZABETH
        EMBRACING HENRY

        her face seen over his shoulder.

                    ELIZABETH (hysterically)
                         No, Henry! No! I know what
                         you're thinking! But it's not
                         that, not that!

        DISSOLVE TO:

F-22   INT CASTLE FRANKENSTEIN
        DRAWING ROOM..NIGHT..MED SHOT

        Henry, alone, shows his fear
        and agitation more than he
        permitted himself to do before
        his wife. He walks up and down.
        He pulls at his collar as though
        choking for air. He turns and
        jerks open two long French windows,
        walking out onto the stone veranda
        into the fresh air.

F-23   EXT CASTLE FRANKENSTEIN
        STONE VERANDA..MED SHOT
        HENRY

        pacing up and down.

F-24   EXT CASTLE..STONE VERANDA
        CLOSE SHOT

        We see one end of veranda, show-
        ing stone balustrade running
        across end of veranda and then
        turning at right angles. Beyond
        we see tops of trees, showing
        that the varanda is built up a con-
        siderable distance from ground.

        The Monster's head and shoulders
        appear as he climbs up from below.
        He swings himself over the railing
        and stands, looking fixidly at
        Henry.

        This scene should be played in
        the dim light shed by the lamps
        within streaming thru the French
        windows.

F-25   LONG SHOT..REVERSE ANGLE
        VERANDA

        as seen by Monster. Henry is
        pacing along, his back to Monster.
        Light streams from window on floor
        above just over Henry's head, as
        shutters are thrown open and Eliza-
        beth, in negligee, leans out and
        calls gently to Henry..

                        ELIZABETH
                    Henry, come up - don't leave
                    me alone tonight.

                HENRY   (looking up at her)
                    I'm just coming, darling.

        She withdraws and closes
        window, shutting off light
        from her room. She has not
        seen the Monster. But the
        Monster has seen her.

        Henry turns and comes toward
        CAMERA to reenter drawingroom
        thru French windows. He sees
        the Monster, stops, staring at
        him, paralyzed.

F-26   CLOSE SHOT HENRY

He stands absolutely still,
staring at the Monster. He
thinks this is death. He knows
from past experience that the
Monster is faster, more agile
than he is.

At this moment he thinks of
Elizabeth. He looks up to her
window. It is closed, the blinds
are drawn. Slowly he turns his
head back and stares at the Monster like a bird fascinated by a
snake. He slowly crosses himself

F-27   MED SHOT TERRACE...NIGHT

The Monster is slowly advancing
on Henry, who stands motionless.

F-28   TWO SHOT HENRY & MONSTER

Henry, as a last hope, like a
man with a fierce dog, tries to
dominate the Monster by treating
him as a slave, as we saw him do
after the creation in the first
picture.

                    HENRY   (pointing to stone paving)
                         Down, Slave! Kneel down, you
                         dog! Get down - I am your
                         master!

The Monster stands, a
tower of strength, and a
grin shows itself. He repeats
ironically..

                    MONSTER
                         Master!

He laughs, then angrily
he beats his chest with
his right hand

                         You are dog, you are slave!
                         Frank-en-stein mas-ter now!

Henry recoils a step
astonishment almost overcom-
ing his terror.

                    HENRY
                         Words - speech - who could
                         have taught...?

                    MONSTER   (interrupting, proudly)
                         Frank-en-stein taught him-self.

Henry is struck by the
Monster's use of his
name.

                    HENRY
                         Frankenstein? Oh, God!
                              (he laughs hysterically)
                         You call yourself by my name?

(CONTINUED)

150

                    MONSTER
                         No fa-ther, no mo-ther. You
                         make me. You, Frank-en-stein,
                         so I Frank-en-stein.

                    HENRY   (hysterically)
                         You know, you know! Yes, I made
                         you, my horrible creation, with
                         my own hands, out of dead tissue-

                    MONSTER
                         And then you beat me, you chain
                         me, you burn me.

Henry has been thinking
fast. This creature now
has some rudiments of
reason. It can be talked
with. Anything to gain time.
If he could only get time
to set a trap. He changes
his tone.

                    HENRY
                         I was cruel because you were
                         so strong and at first you
                         understood nothing but blows.
                         Now we can talk. I'm responsi-
                         ble for you - I'll do anything
                         I can for you. You've only to
                         tell me what you want - but not
                         now. Come back here tomorrow.

F-29   CLOSE SHOT HENRY &
        MONSTER..FAVORING MONSTER

A cunning grin comes on
Monster's face.
                    MONSTER
                         I come back - I find men hide-
                         men shoot guns - Franken-stein
                         die!

                    HENRY   (with bitter laugh)
                         So, that brain I put in that
                         skull has learned to think!
                         That brooch! You put it in poor
                         Edward's pocket! What cunning
                         devilry!

                    MONSTER   (give a sort of inhuman
                              laugh. He is pleased with
                              his trick.
                         Yes. I saw man hang from tree.

                    HENRY   (with groan)
                         Why did you kill that poor girl?

                         (CONTINUED)

151

              MONSTER   (with cold fury)
                   All men hate Frank-en-stein.
                   Try kill Frank-en-stein.
                   Frank-en-stein hate! Frank-
                   en-stein kill!

Now he gives orders in
tones of command, while
Henry trembles.

                   When day comes, you go up be-
                   hind town - up, and up, where
                   no men are...

              HENRY
                   Mon Salave!

              MONSTER
                   No man come with you! Frank-
                   en-stein meet you - there!

              HENRY   (anything to get rid of
                      him)
                   If men come with you to kill
                   I hide. Then I wait - I find
                   you - I kill you!

Placing one hand on the
balustrade the Monster,
as nimbly as a boy, vaults
over it and disappears in
the darkness.
DISSOLVE TO:

F-30   INT DRAWING ROOM..NIGHT
       CLOSE SHOT

The room is a blaze of light.
Henry, standing before secretary,
is taking an old-fashioned revolver
from drawer. He examines it to
make sure it is loaded, then slips
it into his pocket.
DISSOLVE TO:

SEQUENCE "G"

G-1   MED SHOT MOUNTAIN PATH
        DAY

        Henry is toiling up to where
        the path ends. The scene is
        desolate. Huge rocks and a few
        scattered trees. To do forward, Henry
        must climb some rocks and proceed
        up a shoulder of the mountains. He
        stops, looks back, looks ahead.
        Then he feels in his pocket for
        his gun. Secure from observation,
        as he stands under an overhanging
        rock, he examines the gun, then he
        looks for a way to climb up the
        rock and starts to do so, climbing
        out of Camera.

G-2   MED SHOT...DAY

        Henry proceeds up shoulder of
        mountain, higher than before.
        This scene is wilder. He stops,
        weary and panting for breath, and
        looks ahead.

G-3   INSERT. STOCK SHOT..DAY
        MOUNTAIN RISING AHEAD

        crowned by snow, glaciers on
        its side.

        NOTE: While we don't play any
        scenes in snow and ice, a shot
        like this will help the illusion;
        most of the picture is laid in the
        Juras, and one shot of the snow
        mountains will show how the Monster,
        is sufficiently inured against cold
        and hunger, could hide against any
        pursuit.

        The scene between Henry and the
        Monster that follows can be conceived
        as taking place high up on the should-
        er of the mountain, but before the
        snow line is reached.

G-4   CLOSE SHOT STEEP ROCK ASCENT

        higher on the mountain. Henry with
        difficulty, is climbing up. Suddenly,
        across the bright sunshine on the
        rock, comes a vast shadow, the shadow
        of the Monster, spread over the rock so
        that by the illusion of perspective it
        looks like that of a colossus. Henry
        sees the shadow and looks up

153

G-5   MED CLOSE SHOT...DAY...
        MONSTER

        standing on top of rock
        looking down at Henry, who
        has stopped climbing, holding
        on by his hands and looking
        up at the figure above him.

        The Monster makes a gesture
        to Henry to come on up and
        Henry starts climbing again.

G-6   MED CLOSE SHOT....DAY
        TOP OF ROCK

        Monster standing as before.
        Henry, having reached the top,
        is standing panting a few feet
        away.

                              HENRY   (with violent determination)
                                   I made you, and now, God help
                                   me, I must atone for it and
                                   destroy you!

        As he says this he pulls
        out old-fashioned revolver
        from hip pocket. This action
        and his words are simultaneous.
        So, almost, is the way Monster's
        leap upon him.

        The monster springs like a cat
        across the rock as Henry is rais-
        ing the gun. It goes off in the
        air as Monster knocks his hand
        up and knocks Henry down with the
        force of his impact. Instantly
        the Monster wrenches the gun from
        Henry's hand and steps back, Henry
        lying bruised and panting on the
        rock.

G-7   CLOSE SHOT MONSTER

        examining gun, rage and triumph
        in his face. He opens the gun
        in the middle. Cartridges fall
        out.

G-8   CLOSEUP REVOLVER

        held open in Monster's hands.
        Monster's snarl is heard as with
        his right hand he twists the gun
        barrel. His strength is such that
        he twists the barrel around until
        the screws break and the gun comes
        apart, the barrel remaining in one
        hand, the butt in the other

F-9   MED CLOSE OF MONSTER

standing, half of the revolver
in each of his hands, Henry
lying on rock. The Monster
raises both hands above his
head and smashes the gun down
on the rock, then he turns to
Henry, takes two steps forward
and stands, one foot planted
forward, looking down at him.

Henry, expecting death, moans
feebly, his last thoughts for
his wife.

                    HENRY
              Elizabeth! Oh, Elizabeth!

The Monster steps back
and with his right hand
he imperiously gestures
Henry to get up.

Henry rises to his feet.
Monster, still silent, points
with outstretched right hand
across the more of less level
rocky surface, indicating that
Henry is to precede him.

Henry, completely at the Monster's
mercy, walks across rock before
him. He looks back. Monster motions
him to go on, then, with shambling
gait and head hung down, the Monster follows.

G-10   MED LONG SHOT ROCKY LEDGE
        ON MOUNTAIN

Henry is walking some distance
ahead of the Monster. He looks
back over his shoulder, and in an
effort to escape he breaks into a
run. He dodges and twists in and
out and disappears behind a rock,
scrambling down.

No sooner has Henry started to run
down than the Monster bounds after
him. The point of this shot is to
indicate the Monster's super-human
agility. Where Henry had had to
scramble, he leaps, his footing as
sure as that of a mountain goat.

G-11   MED SHOT CHASM IN MOUNTAIN

        Henry is crawling across a
        narrow ledge of rock and reaches
        the other side just as the Mon-
        ster bounds in, clears the chasm with
        one flying leap. Henry stumbles to
        his knees. The Monster with one huge
        paw picks him up by the back of the
        neck and gives an inhuman sort of
        laugh. She starts dragging Henry, still
        holding him by the back of the neck,
        back across the shelf of rock that
        spans the chasm.

G-12   EXT CAVE UNDER OVER JUTTING ROCK

        The Monster enters, dragging Henry,
        and flings him roughly down in mouth
        of cave. Henry moans, then sits up
        as Monster takes two steps backward,
        folds his arms and silently looks
        at Henry.

        The sun penetrates the cave, which
        is a natural hole under the rock
        such as used by our stone-age ances-
        tors. The Monster has made this his
        hideout. We see the ashes of his
        fire, the leg and shoulder of a cow,
        raw meat, lying in a corner, bits of
        pine boughs splintered by the Monster's
        hands ready for his fire; two or three
        stolen cloaks heaped up beside the
        fire.

G-13   TWO SHOT HENRY & MONSTER

        Henry is sitting, hopeless, but show-
        ing courage in the face of death; the
        Monster still stands glaring at him.

                             MONSTER
                                 You make me more strong than
                                 you. I cannot make life like you-
                                     (with strangling motion
                                     of his hands)
                                 - but I can kill life!

                        HENRY   (looking up)
                                 Oh God, let me suffer, but let
                                 there be no more innocent vic-
                                 tims!

                        MONSTER   (interrupting)

                                 God! Who is God! I see man,
                                 wo-man, fall on knees - talk
                                 to God

                                 (CONTINUED)

                         HENRY
                              You couldn't understand. God
                              is man's God. God gave life to
                              all men. But I, a man, gave
                              life to you - I am your God!

Up to this point Henry's
mood has been hopeless. Now
to his astonishment the Monster goes on his knees before
him.

                         MONSTER
                              Yes - you hate me - you try
                              kill me - but you my God!

                         HENRY
                              You - pray to me! I hate you,
                              and yet you are mine, you are
                              part of me. I know now how
                              God felt when He made man, and
                              man turned out a filthy mess.
                              He must have hated us. and
                              yet...we were His responsibility

                         MONSTER
                              I come to you who made me -
                              you try kill me. Help me!

                         HENRY
                              There's only one way I could
                              help you, you filthy mass that
                              walks and talks. Remove you
                              from the earth, where you
                              should never have existed. I
                              tried and failed - you were
                              stronger than I, and more cun-
                              ning. But in a queer way you're
                              right. I never thought of it
                              before, but I not only sinned
                              against God and man when I made
                              you, I sinned against you, too.

                         MONSTER
                              I am a-lone - I need friends -
                              I need - love.

                        HENRY   (with disgust and horror_
                              Love! You!

                         MONSTER
                              all men have friends - love -
                              you have mate - wife.

Now he scrambles to his
feet and steps back, the
mood that made him fall on
his knees before Henry changed
to one of imperious command as
he flings an order in Henry's
face.

                              (CONTINUED)

MONSTER
>You made me - make me wo-man
>like me!

Henry's face shows his
horror as the Monster
continues..

>You can! You must!

HENRY   (scrambling to his feet,
>   forgetting his own danger
>   in the horror of this pro-
>   posal)
>So that's why you came back -
>that's why you forced me to
>follow you here! Do you think
>I'd go thru all that horror
>again - not for all the devils
>in hell!

MONSTER
>Every man - every beast - has
>mate. Only Frank-en-stein
>a-lone.

HENRY
>I wouldn't do it anyway, but
>I can't!

MONSTER
>Men will hate her as they hate
>me - but she not hate me, she
>not afraid. She love me, I
>love her.

HENRY
>I tell you what you ask is
>impossible!

MONSTER
>You make her, I take her with
>me, far from all men - in mount-
>ains where no men live - in woods
>she live with me - we will never
>kill - never see you or any
>men again - no more hate - only
>love!

HENRY
>I see what you mean - give you
>a mate like yourself, and you
>promise to stop these murders
>and live with her in forests,
>deserts, mountains...
>   (He broods a moment)
>I loathe you - you killed my
>father and those innocent people.
>And yet, there is a sort of
>justice in what you ask. But
>I couldn't do it if I wanted to.
>My notes, my formulas - every-
>thing that made it possible for
>me to bring you to life - they
>were all lost when you escaped!

G-14   CLOSE SHOT MONSTER

He slowly draws from the
inside picket of his jacket
Henry's notebook, a triumphant
grin on his face.

G-15   CLOSE SHOT HENRY

watching him. The notebook is
flung down at his feet. Henry
picks it up, opens it, astonishment in his face as he gasps

                    HENRY
                         The notes of all my experiments - -
                         my dissecting - my filthy work
                         among the dead!

He closes book and looks
up at the Monster.

                         I remember - I put them in the
                         coat I gave you - that coat
                         you still wear!

G-16   TWO SHOT HENRY & MONSTER

                    MONSTER
                         you meant to kill me and put
                         that book in the ground with me.

                    HENRY   (looking at him with awe)
                         How can you know that? You've
                         read it all! Who taught you?
                         Your mind is more than human -
                         just as your body is stronger
                         than any man's!

                    MONSTER
                         You can make mate for Frank-en-
                         stein! Make me wo-man, and
                         I will take her, and not kill
                         you.

                    HENRY
                         No!

                    MONSTER   (cold menace in his tone)
                         I can hide - you will not know
                         when I come - I will kill you.
                         And then, - I will take your
                         woman!

Henry looks at him, speechless, and stands silently.
The Monster folds his arms
and keeps his gaze burning on
Henry's face.

DISSOLVE TO:

SEQUENCE "H"

H-1-2-3 CASTLE FRANKENSTEIN
VESTIBULE NEAR DOOR..CLOSE
SHOT...NIGHT

Elizabeth has her arms around
the neck of Henry, who has on
his cloak and hat for departure.
She is trying to hold him back.
The are both in a highly hys-
terical condition.

                    HENRY
                         I can't tell you - don't ask
                         me, my darling - it's for your
                         sake - it won't be long!

                    ELIZABETH
                         But how long, and where are you
                         going?

                    HENRY
                         A few weeks - no more - and then
                         I'll come back to you a new
                         man - and we'll live out our
                         lives here in peace.

Elizabeth is still cling-
ing to Henry. She twists her
head to look behind her to
make sure no servants are
listening, and then says in
a low, intense voice..

                    ELIZABETH
                         It's come back! You've seen it!
                         It killed Justine! Don't leave
                         me!

                    HENRY   (greatly distressed)
                         My darling, my life, I swear
                         to you I'm leaving you to save
                         you, to save myself - it's the
                         only way. Won't you trust me?
                         Won't you believe me?

                    ELIZABETH
                         Yes, yes, but why won't you
                         tell me? It's some horrible
                         secret you're keeping from me!

                    HENRY
                         I can't tell you, I cannot! But
                         I promise you this - that thing
                         will never come back - it will
                         not harm us or anyone ever
                         again - that's why I'm going!

She clings to him, moaning,
and kisses him. Henry,
after the kiss, disengages
himself, pleading with her..

                              (CONTINUED)

160

                              HENRY
                         Don't make me weak. It's for
                         you sake! Remember that!
                         Your sake!

        Dashing tears from his
        eyes, he turns to heavy
        oak door, opens it and
        is gone, closing door
        behind him. Elizabeth rushes
        to door, as if to follow him,
        but her hand on the doorknob,
        her knees give way under her
        and she sinks to the floor
        sobbing.

        DISSOLVE TO:

I-1   CLOSE SHOT DOOR - DAY

       It is an old-fashioned door,
       such as one would expect in
       a provincial medical school,
       not a spic-and-span American
       door. In faded, black letters
       old-fashioned lettering, we read
       on the door:

            "DISSECTING ROOM"

       Dissolve thru door.

I-2   INT. DISSECTING ROOM - DAY
       CLOSE SHOT LIVE FROG

       The frog's eyes blink and
       we see his throat expand
       and contract. Both legs
       of the frog have small white
       bandages around them.

       Wires, apparently inserted
       in frog, lead into a small
       electrical gadget on table.
       A man's hand is moving the
       switch. A light glimmers in
       a sort of galvanometer attach-
       ed to the wires leading into
       the frog. The light is timed
       to flash in time with the expan-
       sion and contraction of the
       frog's throat as it breathes.

I-3   MED. SHOT FROG ON TABLE

       Professor of Anatomy is stand-
       ing behind table working the
       switch to make the frog breath,
       a group of six or eight students
       are standing watching and listen-
       ing to the demonstraton.

                         PROFESSOR OF ANATOMY
                              For this experiment, Gentlemen,
                              I should once have been burned as
                              a wizard. You see that this frog
                              lives - the heart still beats. The
                              slaine solution in the veins, the
                              current properly applied, send blood
                              even into these two legs which you
                              saw me amputate from two other
                              frogs. In a sense, I have there-
                              fore created life.   (CONTINUED

162

STUDENT

Herr Professor, how long will the
frog live?

PROFESSOR

Only so long as the current is
applied, as the injections are
continued. What you see is not
life itself. It is the simulacrum
of life. Now let us apply what
we have learned to the more complex
structure of the human body. This
way, gentlemen, please.

The Professor moves off,
followed by students.

CUT TO:

I-4   INT. DISSECTING ROOM
       MED. SHOT. - DAY

The Professor is lecturing
behind another slab. The
light isn't so good on this
side of the room, and the
students are grouped between
the object on the slab and
the camera so that we don't
see it.

PROFESSOR

In the case of the human heart, whose
more complex structure you are now
studying, the problem is the same
the detail infinitely more complex.
But do not mistake me. Could we
make his heart beat again, it would
beat only so long as our apparatus
continues to function - the prin-
ciple of life itself is for the
present, perhaps forever, beyond
our grasp.

DISSOLVE TO:

I-5   EXT. DISSECTING ROOM DOOR-
       NIGHT - MED. CLOSE SHOT.

At first, darkness. A dark
lantern is flashed on the
door, and we read again:

"DISSECTING ROOM"

By the light of the lantern
we see the misshappen dwarf,
Fritz, Henry's accomplice
in the creation of the Monster in the first picture.

(CONTINUED)

I-5   (CONTINUED)

He has with him a bag, which
he puts down, trains lantern
on it, opens it, takes out
chisel and hammer. He slips
the chisel in the crack of
the door, hammers at it, and
starts to pry door open. We
hear the sound of splintering
wood, or breaking lock, as we

DISSOLVE TO:

I-6   INT. HENRY'S LABORATORY - MED.
       SHOT - NIGHT.

NOTE: This is the same scene as
that which witnessed the creation
of the Monster in the first picture. A ruined medieval castle
on the top of a mountain spur,
part of it reconstructed by
Henry into a laboratory.

Our problem is, not only to vary
the dramatics of this new creation to make it seem unlike the
first one, but also to make the
business and apparatus of the
creation of the woman as different
as we can from the first picture.
On the other hand, Henry would
obviously to some extent have to
repeat the process. The audience
will expect him to hoist the body
about to receive life up above the
lab itself as he did before. Otherwise by starting his work at an
earlier period, we make it all seem
different, because all we saw in
the first picture in the lab of
the creation itself was the body
put together and sheeted over ready
to receive life.

All this means that the props
in this big room should be the
same as they were before, plus
the new stuff called for in the
various shots that follow.

We want a window where we had none
before. Some of the electrical
machinery used before is called
for, as described in what follows.
The roof should be constructed as
before, so that half of it slides
back, controlled by levers, like
the rounded dome of an astronomical
observatory.

Henry, in a white apron, back to
camera, is working, intense and
nervous, over something on a slab.
He throws down scalpel in disgust.

(CONTINUED)

164

throws a rubber sheet over the
stuff on the slab, and turns and
calls:

                    HENRY

                         Fritz! Take this out and bury it!

Dwarf scuttles into
scene.

                    HENRY
                         Useless! Perfectly useless! Once
                         degeneration sets in the tissues...
                              (he turns on dwarf)
                         I must have a heart that's healthy -
                         one that has stopped beating for
                         only a few hours!

Fritz mumbles and shakes
his head.

                    HENRY

                         Any fool can get this dissecting
                         room material - You know what I
                         want - find it for me! For the
                         major organs I need a victim of
                         accidental death - the heart must
                         be sound!

               FRITZ   (mumbling)

                         Accidental death - a thousand crowns
                         you promised me.

                    HENRY

                         A thousand crowns, if you bring me
                         what I want, and help me with -
                         the experiment.

                    FRITZ

                         I'll try again, Master.

Henry, paying little at-
tention to him, now swings
away and flings himself down
at a table where he begins
examining some tissue with
microscope and making notes.

DISSOLVE TO:

I-1   STREET IN GOLDSTADT - NIGHT
        MED. CLOSE SHOT.

Corner of two narrow streets
lit by feeble gas light pro-

(CONTINUED)

I-7   (CONTINUED)

        jecting from iron bracket
        fastened in corner house at
        street intersection.

        Fritz is standing at corner.
        He looks up street past camera
        as though he saw someone coming,
        gives a quick look back against
        wall just around corner, where
        he lies in wait, unseen by the
        approaching victim.

        CUT TO:

I-8   MED. SHOT. STREET.

        leading at right angles from
        the corner where Fritz is hid-
        ing. The street is deserted,
        except for a young woman who
        is walking along, shawl over
        her head.

        CAMERA PULLS BACK SHOWING
        ANGLE OF STREET CORNER so
        that we see waiting Dwarf
        and approaching woman.

        She walks to corner, Dwarf
        springs out from around cor-
        ner, garrotes her with a rope.
        The cry she starts to give dies
        into a gurgle as the rope
        tightens. Just a flash of this.

        DISSOLVE TO:

I-9   INT. LAB - MED. SHOT

        On a large table is a glass
        retort. In this is a dead
        object submerged in liquid.
        Tubes lead from this object
        to another retort. Electric
        wires connected with the tubes
        lead to a sort of galvanometer
        fastened on bench, which keeps
        lighting up with faint light
        as the current pulses.

        Henry is leaning eagerly over
        the table, watching first the
        heart in the first retort, then
        the telltale flashes on the
        galvanometer.

        Henry's scientific enthusiasm
        when things are going right is
        intended to contrast with his
        despair and agony previously when
        he had time to reflect on what he
        had done. When he is the man of
        pure science, as now, he forgets   (CONTINUED)

166

everything but his results.
He is a split personality.

                              HENRY

                              It's beating perfectly! Pulsing,
                              just as in life - now if I can
                              only keep it that way until...

A thought suddenly strikes
him and he breaks off and
turns quickly on the Dwarf,
a look of suspicion in his
face.

CAMERA PULLS BACK to take
in Dwarf, who is watching
Henry and the retorts.

                         DWARF

                              It was a fresh one, Master.

                    HENRY
                              There were marks about that cadaver's
                              neck!

                    DWARF   (in wheedling tones)

                              I paid the gendarme fifty crowns -
                              it's only fair you should add that
                              to my wages.

                    HENRY

                              What gendarme? How about those
                              marks on the neck?

                         DWARF

                              Her husband found her with her
                              lover and strangled her, sir.
                              I paid the police to let me -

But Henry dismisses the
subject, merely snapping out:

                         HENRY

                              You shall have your fifty crowns!

He turns back eagerly to
the apparatus on the bench.

DISSOLVE TO:

I-10   INT. LAB - NIGHT - MED.
       CLOSE SHOT.

Henry is working over his last
preparations. A lamp stands on
a crude table made by putting a
plank across two sawbucks. With
a pen, he is calculating formulae.   (CONTINUED)

I-10   (CONTINUED)

       The black note book that the
       Monster formerly carried is
       open before him.

       Henry looks more wan and hag-
       gard than in previous shots.
       His incessant work and mental
       strain have exhausted him. He
       falls asleep at his work, drops
       his pen, his head sinking forward
       on his forearms.

       CUT TO:

I-11   CLOSE SHOT. LARGE WINDOW
       LAB - MOONLIGHT - SHOOTING
       FROM WITHIN.

       Monster's hands appear stretched
       up from below, grasping iron
       bars. His face and shoulders
       follow as he pulls himself up.
       He glares inside. Then, using
       his enormous strength, he sets
       himself to twisting and pulling
       out the iron bars, yanking them
       apart and throwing them down
       outside one after another as
       though they were rubber.

       Having torn out enough bars to
       climb through, he takes bar and
       smashes the glass in the window
       within. Then he climbs through
       and springs to the floor.

       DUT TO:

I-12   MED. SHOT. HENRY - ASLEEP.

       his head slumped down on table,
       as before. The noise has not
       awakened him. The Monster strides
       into camera, seizes Henry's
       shoulder and shakes him roughly.
       Henry looks up at first he thinks
       this is only a familar nightmare.
       He waves his hand as if to dis-
       sipate the horrid vision. But as
       he wakes fully and sees it is real
       he leaps to his feet, taking a few
       steps back.

                  MONSTER (pointing sternly over towards
                             slabs, apparatus, machinery,
                             which we see dimly in back-
                             ground)

             Work!

       (CONTINUED)

I-12   (CONTINUED)

Henry looks around, looks up
and sees the window with the
bars torn out and the glass
smashed, and says, grimly:

                        HENRY

                            So, I thought you would follow me!

                    MONSTER

                            While you rode in the valleys, I
                            came after you. I climbed along
                            the rocks, high up -

                    HENRY
                            Why have you broken in here? I'm
                            keeping my promise. You shall have
                            your mate - but a man must sleep!

                    MONSTER

                            Not sleep. Work! Give me my wo-
                            man, and then you can sleep.

        CUT TO:

1-13   INT. LAB. MED. CLOSE SHOT DOOR.

        The door pens and the Dwarf comes
        in. He stops, terror in his face,
        as he sees the Monster standing
        talking to Henry.

        CUT TO:

I-14   MED. SHOT - MONSTER - DWARF
        HENRY

        He recognizes his old enemy of
        the first picture, who tortured
        him with whip and fire. He
        steps toward him with a menacing
        animal-like growl. The Dwarf,
        is gibbering. Henry steps for-
        ward to interfere.

                        HENRY   (to Monster)

                            Let him alone - I can't do this
                            for you without him to help me!

        This stops Monster, who with
        a final growl of rage at
        dwarf, turns back to Henry.

                        MONSTER

                            I go as I came, but I wait, and I
                            watch. Work!
        He half raises a huge fist
        in menace as a threat against
        Henry if Henry lets him down,   (CONTINUED)

I-14   (CONTINUED)

         and turns back toward window

         CUT TO:

I-15   CLOSE SHOT WINDOW

         Monster vaults up through it as
         easily as a gymnast.

         DISSOLVE TO:

I-16   EXT. LAB. FULL SHOT -
         NIGHT.

         It is the half-ruined feudal
         castle on a hill of the first
         picture, used by Henry for his
         laboratory.

         A man is toiling up towards
         the door along a path.

         CUT TO:

I-17   MED. CLOSE SHOT - OUTER
         DOOR OF RUINED CASTLE.

         Father Gerard is banging the
         iron knocker on the outer door.
         He turns and he sees the Mon-
         ster slink by him, coming along
         side of stone wall, and dis-
         appears into the shadow. He
         rattles the knocker again.

         DISSOLVE TO:

I-18   INT. LAB - MED. SHOT

         Father Gerard and Henry are in
         the middle of a tense argument.
         The Priest is pleading with
         Henry. Henry, the climax of
         his work approaching, is exalted
         by scientific enthusiasm, as
         well as convinced that the Mon-
         ster will kill him and Elizabeth
         if he does not go on.

                    FATHER GERARD

                         My Son, my Son, it was this very
                         mortal sin for which you asked
                         absolution!

                    HENRY   (with a wild laugh)

                         Yes, and you didn't believe me-
                         you thought it was a delusion -
                              (CONTINUED)

                              170

> HENRY   (CONTINUED)
>
>> Well, now you say you've seen the
>> Monster yourself. You see that
>> window?
>>   (pointing)
>> He paid me a little visit! So
>> Elizabeth sent you, eh? Go, tell
>> her I'm coming back to her soon!
>
> FATHER GERARD
>>   (looks around him at all the tables,
>>   retorts and instruments)
>>
>> This is the very laboratory of
>> Satan! This unholy work must not
>> go on!
>
> HENRY
>
>> Is there any law against experi-
>> ments with dead tissue? My
>> colleague, Doctor Hartman, has
>> killed rabbits, frogs, and
>> brought them back to life, grafting
>> sewing, galvanising...
>
> FATHER GERARD
>
>> Have you forgotten those murdered
>> innocents? Your strangled father?
>> Those crimes are on your soul,
>> and now you will commit worse...
>
> HENRY   (interrupting)
>
>> I told you this creature is my
>> responsibility - not God's.
>> He's mine - he's part of me!
>> By the horror he inspires, he is
>> cut off from all men. There is
>> justice in what he asks. I give
>> him a companion, a wife. Can I
>> do less than God did for Adam?
>> There will be no more murders
>> when I give him ...

Henry rushes hysterically over
to Father Gerard and grabs him
by the arm, CAMERA FOLLOWING,
drags him against his will into
corner.

>>   .....this!

CUT TO:

1-19   CORNER OF LAB - MED. SHOT

Now we see the various com-
ponents of the mate about to
be created more clearly. They
are assembled for the first
time. In the retort previously

>>   (CONTINUED)

seen, the beating heart, attached by tubes and electric
wires to glowing galvamometer,
is seen. Also a brain in a
glass case. The rest of the
body, or sections of bodies
are lying about under rubber
sheets.

We should not actually see any
of the gruesome details, except
the heart and brain, but by
suitable arrangement, the rest
can be suggested - arms, legs,
torso, head - each lump thought
covered, suggesting what it is
by its shape.

                    HENRY
                         You wonder why I fitted up this
                         lonely ruin for my work, high on
                         this crag - I need the mountain
                         lightnings! I can put this thing
                         together - I can make the heart
                         beat, pulse blood through the
                         veins, but the spark of life itself -
                              (pointing up)
                         That comes from up there!

               FATHER GERARD   (pointing up)

                         Yes, you blasphemer, it comes from
                         up there - it comes from God!

               HENRY   (laughs)

                         You point to Heaven -
                              (he points up again)
                         I point to the stratosphere!
                         I'll tell you my secret - why
                         shouldn't I - when this is over,
                         I'll destroy my notes, smash my
                         apparatus! The principle of
                         all life for man and beast and
                         plant is in the cosmic rays that
                         travel from the depths of space -
                         but the envelope of air that they
                         strike weakens them - when the
                         lightning charge the atmosphere,
                         I go up through the air, drag down
                         the germ of life to do my will!
                         I know how it feels to be God! I
                         shall pay for it - but I shall
                         again have my moment of triumph

               FATHER GERARD

                         My son, this is indeed the sin
                         against the Holy Ghost! A fe-
                         male monster! Are you trying to
                         create a race of devils to make
                         war on God's creatures? They will
                         breed these two! You will people
                         the world with monsters!   (CONTINUED)

I-19   (CONTINUED - 2)

         Father Gerard almost screams
         these last two sentences, and,
         beside himself at the sacrilege
         about to be committed, seizes
         an electric working lamp and
         raises it above his head.

         CUT TO:

I-20   CLOSE SHOT. GERARD BESIDE
         RETORT CONTAINING HEART.

         Father Gerard, the heavy
         electric light standard
         held in his hands above his
         head, is about to bring it
         down, smash the retort and
         ruin Henry's work.

         Henry, a mad light blazing
         in his eyes, just in time
         springs into scene, AS CAMERA
         PULLS BACK, gets one arm around
         Father Gerard's neck and jerks
         him back, the light standard
         crashing harmlessly to the
         floor. Father Gerard sprawls
         on the floor.

                                   HENRY   (standing over him)

                                        So, you would ruin my work! That
                                        thing that's taken my name, broken
                                        my will, made me its creature,
                                        it would kill me - it would kill
                                        Elizabeth - if I should fail!

         During this speech,

         CUT TO:

I-21   MED SHOT IN. LABORATORY

         Father Gerard, struggling to
         his feet, back across room
         towards the door, convinced that
         a devil has entered into Henry.
         He mutters, therefore, the exorcism
         of the Church against evil spirits,
         continually crossing himself.

                                   FATHER GERARD
                                        (we don't hear the actual Latin
                                        words, we merely gather that it
                                        is some sort of spell)

                                        Retro me, Sathanas! Adjuro ergo
                                        te, draco nequiniasime, in nomine
                                        agni immaculati....

         During this the Dwarf opens
         the door.

                                              (CONTINUED)

173

                                    DWARF   (excitedly)

                                    Storm, Master - a great storm
                                         (he points)
                                    Over the mountains - it will be
                                    on us soon!

                                    HENRY   (galvanized into activity)
                                         Get him out of here!
                                              (he points to Father Gerard.
                                              The Dwarf seizes Father
                                              Gerard's arm.)
                                         The kites! Get them ready! Send
                                         them up when the wind rises!
                                         Hurry!, hurry!

          CUT TO:

I-22   MED. CLOSE SHOT. HENRY

          throwing the last of the above
          words over his shoulder, as
          he hurries to his tables and
          retorts, where the fragments
          of the mate are assembled. He
          picks up retort containing
          beating heart, carries it gingerly
          to a small slab under which is
          a quadrangular shape, which may
          be a woman's torso. As he
          starts to pick up the rubber
          sheet covering this,

          LAP DISSOLVE.

SEQUENCE "J"

J-1   EXT. LABORATORY....FULL SHOT
       NIGHT

       The sky is now overcast, wind
       howling, heavy storm is raging
       over the distant mountains.
       Distant and continuous lightning
       is seen; far away rumbling of
       thunder.

       A small figure of Father
       Gerard, his cloak whipped
       about him by the wind, is
       seen scurrying down path away
       from laboratory. Rain begins
       to fall in big drops.

       CUT TO:

J-2   EXT. LABORATORY....TOP OF
       ruined tower....full shot

       Two large box kites, built
       like small bi-plane gliders,
       are securely lashed by ropes
       to iron rings.

       The Dwarf is busy undoing
       the ropes that hold kites
       down. From the two kites
       run copper wires to a huge
       windlass on which thousands
       of feet of copper wire are
       wrapped.

       We see all this, and the Dwarf,
       by the distant and frequent
       flashes of lightning. The storm
       is drawing closer, the wind is
       wilder, the thunder louder.

       CUT TO:

J-3   CLOSE SHOT...TOP OF TOWER

       The Dwarf has his hand on a huge
       lever which he is pulling back with
       difficulty. As he does so part of the
       oval metal flooring moves back and
       the light from below streams up.
       The Dwarf goes on his knees and
       looks over edge of chasm that has
       opened up, down into Henry's lab.

       CUT TO:

175

J-4   LONG SHOT...INT. LAB.

        seen from above, as by Dwarf,
        Henry has now assembled and
        pieced together the different
        parts of the body. We see on
        a sort of stretcher, which is
        arranged so that it can be
        hoisted up to the roof, the
        assembled body. Beside the
        stretcher stands a table. On
        the table are the retorts, gal-
        vanometer, etc. connected with
        the beating heart, previously
        seen.

        Henry is bending over the stretcher
        as though he had just completed
        putting in the heart, and connect-
        in it up.

        NOTE: Henry's figure should be
        tiny and what he is doing hardly
        observable. We don't want to draw
        too much attention to gruesome
        detail, or to the practical
        difficulty of such a job.

        Henry looks up, sees that the top
        of the lab is rolled back, cups
        his hands to his mouth and shouts:

                        HENRY
                The wire! Drop down the wire!

        CUT TO:

J-5   TOP OF TOWER

        Dwarf climbs up, steps over to
        windlass and presses a lever which
        causes it to rotate clockwise. He
        seizes the end of copper wire, which
        begins to pay out from windlass and
        lowers it into lab.

        CUT TO:

J-6   LONG SHOT FROM TOWER

        showing Henry's hand up, waiting to
        catch the wire which is slowly com-
        ing down from above. He grabs the
        end of it, and shouts:

                        HENRY
                Stop the windlass!

                    (CONTINUED)

176

J-6   CONTINUED

    Henry now connects wire in
    some way to the body, we don't
    quite see what he does. Too
    much detail about what he is
    doing down here would be bad,
    because it would arouse indredul-
    ity. Hence, no close shots, or
    anything that can be made out
    clearly regarding Henry's final
    proceedings with the body.

    Henry adjusts wire - dashes over
    to side of wall and we see him
    climbing the rungs of a sort of
    ladder built in the wall.

    CUT TO:

J-7   MED. CLOSE SHOT...LAB WINDOW

    shooting from inside lab. There
    is darkness without. A crash of
    lightning comes. By the flash
    of lightning we see the Monster's
    face eagerly peering within, his
    hands clutching for support to
    two iron bars on each side of the
    window - the center iron bars were,
    of course, pulled out by him on his
    previous visit.

    CUT TO:

J-8   MED. SHOT..TOP OF TOWER

    Lightning, wind and thunder.

    Dwarf is holding down one of the
    two kites which seems to be about
    to be torn from its mooring by the
    wind.

    Henry's head and shoulders appear
    as he climbs up from end of ladder
    and joins dwarf.

                    HENRY
              Now, up with the kites!

    He is exalted - an entirely dif-
    ferent Henry from the man we have
    known throughout the picture -
    only the scientific miracle that
    he hopes to accomplish matters to
    him now, and as he stands there
    with the elements raging about him,
    he is like a man inspired.

    He rushes to cast loose one of the
    kites, while the Dwarf busies himself
    with the other.   (CONTINUED)

J-8   CONTINUED

These kites are obviously
no children's toys - they are
carefully made of pigskin, which
looks like parchment, with struts
of aluminum. And each is some four
feet in wing-spread.

As the ropes that are holding them
are cast off, each man struggles
with his kite, having difficulty in
holding it. Each lifts his kite and
launches it in the wind. The wind
tears them away.

CUT TO:

J-9   CLOSE SHOT..WINDLASS

revolving rapidly, anti-clockwise,
paying out the thing copper wire
attached to each of the kites. From
under the windlass we see the other
end of the wire that stretches down
from the roof to the body.

NOTE: For the credibility much depends
on windlass, apparently with ball-
bearings, running easily and efficient-
ly, and using very thin wire. Any sort
of heavy apparatus would obviously
not work.

CUT TO:

J-10   LONG SHOT..TOP OF TOWER

The two kites, torn by the wind,
are borne into the sky on the wings
of the storm. By the flashes of
lightning we see the kites tearing
up, Henry and Dwarf's small figures on the roof, rushing about, the
windlass revolving paying out the wire.

CUT TO:

J-11   LONG SHOT...INTO LAB

looking down from top of tower.
Henry is climbing down ladder
inside as fast as possible to get back
to his work with the body.

CUT TO:

J-12   CLOSE SHOT...WINDOW

Monster's face, seen by flashes of
lightning, watching the work pro-
ceeding within.

CUT TO:

J-13   MINIATURE SHOT...SKY

One of the kites in the midst
of the storm revealed by flash of
lightning.

CUT TO:

J-14   INT. LAB...MED. SHOT

Henry is working over the form on
the slab, now entirely covered with
rubber sheet. The wires leading
from the kites dangling down from
the opening in the roof are now
attached to electrodes and fastened
around the body.

There are two metal globes standing
on top of standards, now placed, one
at head, one at foot of the metal
table on which the body is laid.

Branch wires from the wire dangling
from roof to body are seen extended
at right-angles, from the main wire,
attached to the two globes.

Henry rushes to wall, throws switch.
The moveable stretcher on which the
body is laid rises some four feet. The
body is now suspended equally distant
between the two globes.

CUT TO:

J-15   MINIATURE SHOT...SKY FLASH

Kite in midst of storm. A great
flash of lightning.

CUT TO:

J-16   INT.LAB...BODY SUSPENDED AS
        BEFORE

The lightning flash blows out the
fuses, plunging room in darkness
and is followed by a terrific clap
of thunder.

The two globes are artificial lightning
producers, and now commence to throw huge
sparks, crackling and sizzling, from one
to the other globe, the sparks apparently
passing through the body.

The idea here is to suggest that the
electrical discharges carrying the cosmic
rays are coming down the wires from the
kites in the sky, so that it is the trapped
lightning itself which is both infusing
the body and leaping back and forth between the globes.   (CONTINUED)

179

J-16   CONTINUED

All the previous business with the
globes, wires, kites, etc. should
be thought out with the view of
conveying this impression.

CUT TO:

J-17   EXT. TOP OF TOWER...CLOSE SHOT

The Dwarf is attending to the paying
out of the wires from the windlass
to the two kites. They have now risen
to their maximum height, for the wire
has all gone from the spindle, and the
Dwarf stops the windlass from turning.

As he does so, the Monster's head appears above the parapet. The Monster
has pulled himself up the side of the
outside wall, from the window where
we saw his face before, to see what is
going on up there. The Dwarf does not
see him. Dwarf hurries to the edge
of the steel roof opened previously
and peers down.

CUT TO:

J-18   LONG SHOT INT. LAB

Shooting down from top of tower.
As lights are out down there we
merely see the artificial lightning
discharges leaping back and forth
between the two globes lighting up
Henry and the corpse on the suspended
stretcher with the unearthly flashes.

Henry cups his hands to his mouth and
shouts up to the Dwarf. We barely hear
his words through the storm.

                    HENRY
                         Ready! It's coming up!

                              CUT TO:

J-19   INT. LAB...MED.SHOT

Henry, by wall, pulls a lever. The
stretcher on which the corpse lies
slowly starts to ascend towards the
roof. We see it hovering in the half-
darkenss, still lit up by the great
sparks flying back and forth between
the globes. These sparks look like
miniature lightning flashes, which they
are.

NOTE: This stunt is being done now on a
big scale at Cal. Tech. and can be du-
plicated on any scale desired.
CUT TO:

180

J-20   TOP OF ROOF...MED. CLOSE SHOT

         The Dwarf in kneeling, looking
         down. The Monster, unseen by Dwarf,
         is standing behind him, also looking
         down. Slowly the stretcher contain-
         ing the corpse, hoisted by cables,
         appears in opening. It swings there
         a moment.

         CUT TO:

J-21   MINIATURE SHOT SKY..KITE

         Seen by another flash of lightning,
         which carries over to

J-22   FLASH...CLOSE SHOT...TOP OF TOWER

         The corpse is hanging there and this,
         with Monster and Dwarf, are momentarily
         seen in flash.

         The wires attached to the kites are
         observable attached to the body, lead-
         ing to windlass, and then up to the sky
         where the kites are straining in storm.

         CUT TO:

J-23   INT. LAB....FULL SHOT

         shooting up from floor. Henry is
         peering up, with hand on lever. We
         see, revealed by a lightning flash,
         the stretcher containing corpse swing-
         ing in the opening of the roof, the
         Dwarf's face peering down.

         Henry pulls lever and this starts
         stretcher coming down again.

         CUT TO:

J-24   EXT. TOP OF DOOR...MED. CLOSE SHOT

         Dwarf, on knees, peering down in
         lab, Monster standing behind him
         looking down. Dwarf gets up and turns.

         The center of the storm has now passed
         on. Lightning flashes continue to rapid-
         ly succeed one another, but they are now
         more distant, and the thunder not so loud.
         By the light of these intermittent flashes
         we play what follows.

                                    (CONTINUED)

As the Dwarf rises and turns
he sees the Monster behind him.
He gibbers in terror. The Monster
stretches out his long arms and
grabs the Dwarf by the neck, with
both hands. There is a brief and
futile struggle, the Monster picks
him up and throws him over the edge
of the parapet. The Dwarf disappears
with a scream.

DISSOLVE TO:

J-25   INT. LAB - CLOSE SHOT
         HEAD OF MATE

         On stretcher, Henry's
         hands seen removing cloth
         from her face.

         The face has a strange, in-
         human, terrible beauty.
         Around the neck is a bandage
         lightly laid on. Henry's
         hands lift the bandage. We
         see a flash of a red scar,
         criss-cross stitches. Henry's
         hands lay the bandage back
         around neck.

         CUT TO:

J-26   INT. LABORATORY
         MED. CLOSE SHOT HENRY

         Bending over the face on the
         stretcher, intently watching
         it for signs of life.

         The lab is now lit by two or
         three oil lamps grouped around
         the stretcher, prepared by
         Henry for such an emergency
         as did arise - the blowing out
         of his light fuses by the elec-
         trical discharges brought down
         from the clouds. Thus the
         lighting of this scene is made
         more mysterious. The form on
         the stretcher is well lit, but
         the rest of the lab is either
         dark of filled with strange
         shadows.

         CUT TO:

J-27   CLOSE SHOT TOP OF TOWER

         The Monster, on his knees, is
         peering down through the open
         dome.

         CUT TO:

J-28   LONG SHOT INT. LABORATORY
         AS SEEN BY MONSTER ABOVE.

         Henry is doing something, we
         can't quite see what, leaning
         over the body. (This shot is put
         in to get the effect of the New
         and weird lighting in the lab,
         seen from above,)

         CUT TO:

J-29   INT. LAB. CLOSE SHOT
        BODY ON STRETCHER

        The face in unveiled as before,
        Henry is applying a small vial
        to lips.

        CUT TO:

J-30   CLOSEUP MATE'S HEAD &
        SHOULDERS.

        The eyes gradually open.
        Vacant at first, they grad-
        ually focus in an intense
        stare. They seem to contain
        depths of unfathomable mystery.

        CAMERA PULLS BACK showing
        Henry, straightening up from
        bending over face, then with
        a low gasp of triumph, he sets
        himself with flying fingers to
        unfasten the buckles and straps
        which hold the Mate on the
        stretcher. Now he hastens be-
        hind her head, slowly raising
        her, lifting her shoulders to
        a sitting posture. He steps back
        to see what will happen next.

        CUT TO:

J-31   CLOSE SHOT MATE

        Sitting on stretcher. Never
        taking her eyes from Henry,
        she slowly moves her head
        back and forth. She works
        her jaw muscles a little.
        She raises her right arm slowly,
        opens her hand, looks down at
        it, then she looks up at Henry
        again. Henry now farefully lifts
        her feet, slowly pulls them around,
        pivoting her body, and puts them
        on the floor. Then he takes her
        by left arm, gently urging her
        to rise. She does so, slowly,
        her hinges moving like a mech-
        anical doll's as if they creaked
        a little.

        Now she is standing. Henry drops
        her arms and moves back out of
        camera.

        CUT TO:

J-32   CLOSE SHOT MATE

        Standing. She wears a simple
        white garment that falls to
        her feet; cascade of fold hair
        ripples down over her shoulders
        to the waist.   (CONTINUED)

184

J-32   CONTINUED

Slowly she extends her arms,
each arm at an angle of thirty
degrees from her body, and
looks at one and then the other.
She trows her head back and
takes one or two deep breaths
as though trying her lungs.

CUT TO:

J-33   MED. CLOSE SHOT HENRY
        AND MATE

Henry stretches out his arms
to her, encouraging her to
walk, as one teaching a child.
She doesn't understand at first.
She stands looking at him in
amazement. He shows her. He
puts one foot carefully forward,
then plants his other foot in
front of that. The Mate gets
the idea. She brings forward
one leg, stands, swaying a
little, then the other leg.

Henry moves back, still motion-
ing her on. After two or three
steps she finds she can walk.
Her eyes on her Creator, she
smiles for the first time.
In walking, however, in all
movements of her hands, her
head or her body she displays
extreme awkwardness, almost as
though she were put together on
wires. Like a new born child
she has to learn the mechanism
of the body.

She tries to walk again, but the
coordination is wrong and she
stumbles. Henry jumps in and
seizes her. She throws her arms
around his neck and clings to him.
CUT TO:

J-34   CLOSE SHOT HENRY AND MATE

Mate is clinging to Henry, looking into his eyes, s amile on her
lips. Her attitude towards Henry
is that of a tiny puppy towards its
master - trusting dependence.

CUT TO:

J-35   CLOSE SHOT WALL OF LABORATORY

The Monster, half way down ladder,
is clinging to rung with one hand,
his body twisted around, watching
Henry and the mate.
CUT TO:

J-36   MED. LONG SHOT AS SEEN
          BY MONSTER

          Mate is clinging to Henry
          for support.

          CUT TO:

J-37   MED. CLOSE SHOT LADDER

          Monster scurrying down
          ladder to floor.

          CUT TO:

J-38   MED. SHOT LABORATORY

          The Monster, pathetically
          eager, timidly approaches
          his Mate.

          She does not see him. She
          is watching Henry, who has
          released her and stepped
          back a few paces. Henry is
          watching the two of them.
          Monster, like a bashful
          school-boy, stretches out
          an arm towards Mate, but
          is too wrought up for speech.
          Henry makes a gesture for
          the Mate to look to one side,
          and she slowly turns.

          CUT TO:

J-39   MED. CLOSE SHOT MONSTER
          AND MATE

          Monster holding out his arms.
          She turns slowly and for the
          first time sees the Monster.
          Her reaction to him is the
          same as that of everyone
          else - horror.

          CUT TO:

J-40   CLOSEUP MATE

          Horror in her face. She covers
          her face with her hands to shut
          out the dreadful sight.

          CUT TO:

J-41   CLOSE SHOT MONSTER

          He drops his arms. Slowly
          realization that this creature
          made for him, fears and hates
          him, too, comes into his face.

          CUT TO:

J-42   MED. SHOT HENRY, MATE
        AND MONSTER

        Mate turns away from Monster,
        crosses to Henry, clings to
        him for protection, with
        frightened glances over her
        shoulder at Monster.

        CUT TO:

J-43   CLOSE SHOT MATE

        Clinging to Henry, looking
        back at Monster, then up at
        Henry with plea for protection.

        Henry's face is a mixture of
        emotions. This refult of his
        experiment is a surprise to him.
        He doesn't know what to do, and
        looks helplessly at Monster,
        as Monster's roar of mingled pain
        and rage comes over.

        CUT TO:

J-44   MED. CLOSE SHOT MONSTER

        Dashing into scene and tearing
        Mate away from Henry. He picks
        her up in his huge arms, as Henry
        starts to back away, and stands
        holding her. She gives a pro-
        testing scream, but Monster claps
        hand over her mouth.

        Henry's one idea now is to get
        rid of them both. He is hysterical.
        He rushes to the door of the lab
        and throws it open and shouts
        back at Monster.

                        HENRY
                Take her! She's yours -
                I made her for you!

        Monster, carrying Mate,
        shambles to door.

        CUT TO:

J-45   MED SHOT STAIRWAY

        Henry, carrying lantern, comes
        down dark stone stairway, fol-
        lowed by Monster carrying Mate.

        CUT TO:

J-46   MED. CLOSE SHOT DOOR OF
        RUINED CASTLE

        His lantern on stone flagging,
        Henry is pulling back the   (CONTINUED)

J-46   CONTINUED

iron bolts. He flings open
the door and steps back. He
almost shouts at Monster.

                    HENRY
          I've kept my word - keep yours!

The Monster, carrying Mare,
staggers through door, out
into the open. Henry following him. Without a single look
back, or paying any attention
to Henry, the Monster strides
off.

CUT TO:

J-47   LONG SHOT EXT. RUINED CASTLE
        MOONLIGHT

The storm has now passed.
The Monster, carrying Mate's
white form, is seen in the
moonlight in foreground
striding along towards a rising
shoulder of mountain.

Before him, steeply rising
above him, the Mountain, pine
forests and rock ledges.

CUT TO:

J-48   EXT. RUINED CASTLE

Lantern, sitting on flagging
within, lights scene without.
Henry, a few steps outside door
is standing watching the receding Monster with his burden.
He turns to re-enter castle. As
he does so his foot stubles.

CUT TO:

J-49   EXT. CASTLE - CLOSE SHOT

Shattered body of Dwarf is
seen. Henry is looking down
at it with horror. Henry turns
and runs through door.

CUT TO:

J-50   INT. LAB. MED. SHOT

shooting towards door.

Henry appears at door. He is
half laughing, half crying with
hysteria. He staggers over,

                    (CONTINUED)

J-50   CONTINUED

        CAMERA FOLLOWING HIM, looks
        at stretcher, the straps hanging
        down, looks all around at his
        various instruments and apparatus
        and burst into peals of laughter.

        CUT TO:

J-51   CLOSE SHOT HENRY

        His scientific enthusiasm is ended
        with the success of his work. The
        horror of what he has been through
        comes over him. Remorse, fear. Is
        this really the end? Will the Mon-
        ster keep his word? Can he go back
        and live safely with Elizabeth? All
        this is in his mind.

        Completely overwrought, he sinks down
        at the little bench where we saw him
        working at his formulai before, buries
        his head in his arms and sobs.

        DISSOLVE TO:

K-1   INT. MOUNTAIN CAVE
        FULL SHOT

        Shooting from without mouth
        of cave. A fire is burning
        in mouth of cave, by the light
        of which we see the interior.
        Just outside cave is tethered
        a mountain goat, kept by Monster
        for milk. Within cave we see
        bed of pine branches, covered
        by cloaks.

        The Monster enters scene, carry-
        ing now unconscious form of Mate.
        He enters cave, bending down to
        do so. He puts Mate down with
        gentle and tender care, propping
        her up on bed of pine boughs,
        where her back rests against wall.

        CUT TO:

K-2   INT. CAVE - CLOSE SHOT

        Monster kneeling before uncon-
        scious Mate, chafing her hands.
        She opens her eyes, she sees the
        dreaded face close to hers. Her
        eyes dilate with terror. She
        give a thin scream, tries to
        shrink back, puts her forearm
        before her face. Monster scrambles
        back a little from her.

        We play the following scene to
        put across the Monster's desire
        for companionship and love, his
        touching and tragic affection
        for this creature, the only thing
        in the world like himself. It is
        a tragic scene, and it is most
        important that crude sexual desire
        should not be even hinted in it.
        Not to mention censorship, the
        Monster is too repulsive for this
        to be endurable, and anyway he
        wants is love - a real mate - and
        this must come through or the scene
        will be impossible.
        The woman's part in the scene is
        limited to silent expression of
        horror, terror and revulsion, so
        not much can be put in the script
        for her. But given the right
        actress she can put across a great
        deal here.

                        (CONTINUED)

The Monster is now a pitiable
figure. He babbles endearments
and pleas. He digs in embers of
fire and pulls out chunk of
roast meat. He pours some goat's
milk into a gourd. He humbly
approaches Mate with these as
offerings. She shrinks from him
as far as the corner wherein she
is propped will permit.

> MONSTER   (indicating milk)
>   Drink.
>   (indicating meat)
>   Eat. Drink good! Meat good!

He sees she will not and
puts the gourd and meat
down. As he pleads with
her tears run down his
cheeks.

> MONSTER
>   You not fear Frank-en-stein.
>   Not hate. You must love Frank-
>   en-stein. You not know words -
>   I teach you. I find food for
>   you - I find milk - I kill bears
>   for you, you wear furs in cold.
>   Every man have mate - You my
>   mate. You a-lone like me!
>   Men hate you - like me. I
>   work for you - I love you!

As Monster talks she never
takes her horrified eyes off
him and gives little gasps
as he sidles up toward her.

Now he reaches out his great
paw and gently strokes her
white arm. She gives a full-
blooded scream of terror and
hate as she claws at his face
with her fingers, using her
nails like talons. Monster
recoils. He climbs to his
feet, taking two or three steps
backwards and stands looking
at her.

CUT TO:

K-3   CLOSEUP MATE

Her head back, up against the
cave, gasping, sobbing, half
mad with terror and loathing.

CUT TO:

K-4   CLOSEUP MONSTER

His face begins to work   (CONTINUED)

K-4   CONTINUED

convulsively. He gives a
hoarse sob and buries his
face in his hands. He turns
pathetically, with his great
shoulders sunken, and, sobbing,
staggers out into the darkness
past fire, CAMERA FOLLOWING
until his huge hulk is swallowed
up into the shadows.

CUT TO:

K-5   INT. CAVE - CLOSE SHOT MATE

Left alone, she slowly rises.
Again her awkwardness in using
her limbs is manifest. Her one
thought is to escape. She steps
to door of cave, she looks down
at fire. What is this strange
red thing? The warmth is agree-
able. She stretches out her
hands to fire. It feels good
so she naturally wants more. She
reaches her hand down into it,
touching a glowing piece of
wood. She gives a cry of pain
and staggers up, instinctively
putting her burned hand into her
mouth. The, giving the fire as
wide a berth as possible, she
awkwardly walks out of cave and
out of Camera.

DISSOLVE TO:

K-6   PATH OUTSIDE RUINED CASTLE
        NIGHT

Another thunder storm is gathering
over the mountains, distant lightning is seen. Two figures, Father
Gerard and Elizabeth, are seen
toiling up path towards castle.

K-7   MED. SHOT - EXT. CASTLE.
        NIGHT

Elizabeth and Father Gerard are
standing by body of Dwarf. Beyond, the great door leading into
the place stil stands open. Father
Gerard is on his knees ending a
prayer for the dead. He rises

                    ELIZABETH (clutchng his arm)
                        Who is it?

                    FATHER GERARD
                        Poor Henry's assistant.

                        (CONTINUED)

192

                    ELIZABETH (in great alarm)
                        Come!

She grasps Father Gerard's
arm and guides him to open
door. But he wants to keep
her out - this corpse may
mean there is more tragedy
inside.

                    FATHER GERARD
                        My daughter, this tragedy may
                        mean...
                            (he breaks off)
                        Let me go in alone!

                    ELIZABETH
                        If Henry is in there, dead or
                        alive, I am going to him!

They enter open door
hurriedly.

DISSOLVE TO:

K-8   EXT. LAB. - NIGHT
       MED. SHOT HENRY

Standing near the empty
stretcher, confronting
Father Gerard, who is white-
faced and stern. Father
Gerard seems to have just
finished denouncing Henry,
who looks pale and distraught.

                    FATHER GERARD   (in tones like a judge
                                      sentencing a criminal)
                        This is the sin against the
                        Holy Ghost!

He turns away, crossing
himself, as Elizabeth rushes
up to Henry, throws her arms
around his neck and cries
to Father Gerard:

                    ELIZABETH
                        He did it for my sake! This
                        Monster would have killed us all!

                    HENRY   (embracing her, says
                              hysterically)
                        Yes, yes, and now he's promised
                        to keep away from men, from the
                        whole human race, all his life
                        with this creature that I had
                        made for him! That's why I did it!

CUT TO:

K-9   EXT. CASTLE - NIGHT
        MED. LONG SHOT

        The moon is now overcast by
        clouds. The storm over, the
        mountains is approaching, the
        lightning and thunder nearer.

        In a flash of lightning we
        dimly see the Mate approaching
        the door. She walks stiffly,
        rigidly, like a somnambulist.
        Led by some strange instinct,
        like a lost cat, she is return-
        ing, fleeing from the Monster to
        Henry who made her.

        CUT TO:

K-10   INT. LAB. MED. CLOSE SHOT

        Elizabeth is pleading with
        Henry, Father Gerard in the
        background sternly looking on.

                        ELIZABETH
                        Come with us, Henry. Leave this
                        accursed place. If these two
                        foul things you've made come
                        back to Belrive - we'll go away -
                        to America - anywhere, where
                        they can't follow us!

                        HENRY
                        Yes, come, my darling. Come home!

        He takes her arm and turns
        her toward door, but even
        as Henry speaks, on Father
        Gerard's face, as he looks
        towards door, comes an ex-
        pression of amazement and
        horror

        CUT TO:

K-11   INT. LAB. - MED. SHOT

        Shooting towards door.

        Still walking with stiff joints,
        the Mate enters. She looks about
        startled. Are there more of these
        strange beings in the world? Then
        her gaze turns back to Henry. She
        smiles, she gives a little rippling
        laugh of happiness. She holds out
        her arms to him. Slowly she moves
        toward him.

        CUT TO:

K-12   INT. LAB. MED. SHOT

Henry stands stock-still as
the Mate moves up to him.
Father Gerard seizes Elizabeth and pulls her to one side.
The Mate goes to Henry. She
lifts up her burned hand and
shows it to him, then puts it
in her mouth as if to show
that it hurts - the gesture of
an injured child that runs to
its mother.

Father Gerard and Elizabeth
look at each other, speechless,
Then look back to the motionless
Henry and this thing to which
he has given life.

CUT TO:

K-13   MED. LONG SHOT GROUP

Shooting towards door. A
bellow of rage is heard and the
Monster storms in, berserk with
fury, carrying a huge club half
the size of a young tree, a pine
bough that he has splintered
from a tree in the forest.

The Mate sees him and throws her
arms around Henry as if inploring
him for protection.

CUT TO:

K-14   CLOSE SHOT OF MONSTER.

Standing still for one moment,
his mouth open, fire in his
eyes, as he takes in that his
mate has fled from him to Henry.

The great club he carries, if
made from the trunk of a banana
tree, or some similar light hollow
wood, and doctored to look solid,
will help the illusion of the
Monster's super-human strength
as he wields it. It seems a weapon
that no human arm could handle in
such fashion.

The Monster's face contorts.
He raises the club.

CUT TO:

K-15   INT. LAB. MED SHOT

With a bound, the club over his
head, the Monster is on Henry.
We see the club descend, just as
Elizabeth, with a scream, tries
to throw herself in front of Henry
to protect him. Henry falls to the
floor, his skull crushed. Again
the club rises and descends, this
time of Elizabeth's head.

We are lighting this scene with
oil lamps so that there are pools
of light and pools of shadow, and
this tragedy should take place in
shadow, or edge of light pool.

Father Gerard tries to interfere
to save Elizabeth, but the Monster
deals Father Gerard a blow with his
left arm on the chest that knocks
him sprawling back among some of
Henry's instruments.

CUT TO:

The Mate sinks to her knees and
gives a low moan of pain as she
awkwardly picks up Henry's crushed
head and gazes into his face.

The Monster drops his club and with
a low growl of fury and agony reaches
down with his bare hands, grasps
Mate around the throat, staggers up,
dragging her up with him.

Two or three shakes and he flings
her body, her neck broken, across
the floor.

Meanwhile Father Gerard, though
shaken and injured, crawls into
scene, kneeling by bodies of
Henry and Elizabeth, and, crossing himself, commences intoning
the prayer for the dead. He entirely ignores Monster, who turns
and looks down at him.
During these last moments, the
storm has risen. Lightning
flashes, seen through window and
open skylight above, have lit
up the room, the thunder has been
rumbling.

DISSOLVE TO:

196

Some time as passed. The Monster's
fury has given way to despair.
Father Gerard is kneeling, praying
as before. Monster is standing
watching him. The storm without
continues. Lightning flashes
from time to time through the
following light up the room.

                    MONSTER   (to Father Gerard)
                         You talk - to your God?

Father Gerard, who expects
death himself, looks up at
Monster, a lightning flash
showing his calm, fearless
face.
                    FATHER GERARD
                         I talk to my God - and you
                         God.

                    MONSTER   (pointing to Henry's body)
                         I liked - my God!

                    FATHER GERARD
                         My God is your God. The God
                         of all things that live and
                         breathe - of men and beasts -
                         he has pity and pardon even
                         for you.

Now the Priest is imspired.
He realizes what has been
in the Monster's heart. He
continues:
                    FATHER GERARD
                         You sought among men for love
                         and you found only hate. God
                         is love! God loves you!

                    MONSTER   (astonished)
                         God loves - me?
                              (he demands eagerly and
                               violently, beating his
                               breast)
                         Loves Frank-en-stein?

                    FATHER GERARD
                         Yes, God loves even Frankenstein.
                         Ask him to forgive your sins,
                         to bring you peace.

CUT TO:

K-18   CLOSE SHOT MONSTER

His knees shaking under him,
looking at Priest with a great
yearning in his face. He turns,
takes a few steps, bringing him
into a pool of light from one of
the lamps, and looks up through
the open skylight into the storm.

Slowly the Monster's hulk sinks
to his knees. He imitates Father
Gerard and clasps his hands as
he looks up. He murmurs:

                    MONSTER
                 God ... love...peace.

He doesn't know what to
say. But he is praying
as best he can, and the
answer comes.

                    Peace and oblivion.

A blinding flash of lightning
fill the screen, followed by
a terrific crash of thunder.

As the screen clears, the smoke
rolling away, we see the Monster
lying dead. The bolt has wrecked
the instruments, upset the table
near Monster, burned a hole in
the floor, through which a wisp
of smoke is curling up.

CAMERA PULLS BACK SWIFTLY

showng Father Gerard, unhurt,
on his knees, lifting up his
joined hands to Heaven.

                    T H E   E N D

SCREENPLAYS   Finlay McDermid
Universal properties   March 27, 1935

THE BRIDE OF FRANKENSTEIN

Dialogue comparison of shooting script with Balderston script.

SHOOTING SCRIPT   BALDERSTON

Sequence A

Pagixá   Pagaxá

1.   "You know how lightning alarms me," is the only line which has the same wording in both scripts.

2.   "Fire is the most beautiful   "Who said he was burned up
thing in the world! But who said   in a mill?"
the monster was burned to death in it?"

        (Second closest similarity.)

3.   "Those images of horror that   "People, yet unborn, will
you have evoked will bring   lie awake of nights, unable
nightmares to millions of people   to close their eyes because
yet unborn."   of the dreadful visions your
                                       story conjures up."

        Although the trend of the dialogue in the prologue scene is dealing in both cases with the storm without and the story of Frankenstein, the lines, with exception of the above instances and the use of such minor phrases and words as "moral lesson","horror", etc. are not the same.

4 "What living thing could   "Nothing could be left alive
survive that furnace."   in that furnace."

5 "Hans-- are you all right?"   "Hans, are you hurt?"

        The extent of line similarity in mill scene.

        Sequence B

        Extremely minor similarity in certain phrases of long speeches, such as:

1. "This is blasphemy"   "--it is blasphemous and wicked."

2. "--it was like being God."   "I thought myself equal to God."

        SEQUENCE C

N   No similarity

        Sequence D

        Not used at all in Balderston script.

        Sequence X

        The scene in which the Monster enters the hut of the Hermit covers the same ground of establishing friendship as the scene in

Sequence D of Balderston script, except that in shooting script
the Hermit asks and answers his own questions, while the Monster
remains dumb.

SHOOTING SCRIPT   BALDERSTON

"I cannot see you-- I cannot   "If you've come for food or drink
see anything-- you must excuse   you're welcome-- but you must find
me, but I am blind."   it yourself. These old eyes---"

    Extent of line similarity.

    Sequence F

    No similarity.

    Sequence G

    No similarity.

    Sequence H

1. "It is interesting to think,   "For this experiment, Gentlemen,
Henry, that once we should have   I should once have been burned as
been burned at the stake as   a wizard." (The Professor of
wizards for this experiment."   Anatomy performing with frog.)

2. "The human heart is more   "In the case of the human heart,
complex than any other part   whose more complex structure you
of the body."   are now studying----"

3. "This is only the simalcrum   "Only so long as the current is
of life. This action responds   applied. What you see is not life
only so long as the current is   itself. It is the simalcrum of life."
applied."
                                      (These lines in Sequence G of
                                      Balderston script in a different
                                      situation.)

4. "No, this heart is useless-   "Useless! Perfectly useless......
I must have another and it   I must have a heart that's healthy-
must be sound."   one that has stopped beating for
                                      only a few hours!"

5. "What we need is some   "For the major organs I need a
victim of sudden death."   victim of accidental death."

6. "You promised me a   "Accidental death-- a thousand
thousand crowns."   crowns you promised."

7. "I'll try."   "I'll try again, master."

8. "Beating perfectly.. just   "It's beating perfectly! Pulsing,
as in life. If I can only   just as in life-- now if I can only
keep it this way until----   keep it that way until----

9. "It was a very fresh one."   "It was a fresh one, Master."

10; "I gave the gendarme   "I paid the gendarme fifty crowns--"
fifty crowns."

Sequence H (continued)

SHOOTING SCRIPT	BALDERSTON
11. "What gendarme??	"What gendarme? How about those marks on the neck?"
12. "It was a police case."	"I paid the police to let me---"

(An almost identical scene. The scene following, in which the Monster makes Henry continue his work, is similar except that Pretorius' lines are utilized in shooting script and the Dwarf is not threatened by the Monster.)

13. "Work!"	"Work!"
14. "I am exhausted-- I must sleep."	"You shall have your mate-- but a man must sleep!"
15. "No. Work! Finish-- then you sleep."	"Not sleep. Work! Give me my mate, then you can sleep."
16. "The kites! Are the kites ready? Send them up as soon as the wind rises! Hurry! Hurry!"	"The kites! Get them ready! Send them up when the wind rises! Hurry! Hurry!"
17. "The wire! Drop down the wire!"	The same.
18. "All right. Stop the windlass."	"Stop the windlass."
19. "Now up with the kites."	Same.
20. "Ready. It's coming up."	Same.

No similarity in balance of sequence.

Finlay McDermid
March 28, 1935

THE RETURN OF FRANKENSTEIN

File No: 6265

Picture No. _____

General summary of Research:

1. A total of less than thirty lines in a script which contains a good many hundred was supplied by Balderston.

2. Adding to the sum of Balderston action scenes in the shooting script is one utilized in an early Balderston script, later discarded--the rescue by the monster of a girl caught in a mountain torrent.

     a. In Tom Reed's script, however, the Monster frightens, unintentionally, a girl bathing in a lake, then rescues her drowned body. It is possible that this scene was the germ of Balderston's scene.

3. Reed uses the scene in which the Monster sees his image reflected in water.

4. Reed uses the peasant family for whom the Monster works, and the blind grandfather friend.

5. Reed uses the device of having the Monster carry in his pocket instructions written by Frankenstein on the subject of Monster-creating. This device used by Balderston but not by shooting script.

6. Reed and Bloohman use the Mate idea. In both scripts, a threat of harm to Elizabeth moves Frankenstein to create the Mate.

     These are the most important points bearing on the question at hand.

OUTLINE TREATMENT
Universal Property

Finley McDermid
March 28, 1935

THE RETURN OF FRANKENSTEIN

by

L G Blochman

Henry and Elizabeth change their name from Frankenstein to Heinrich, and go into hiding, running a puppet show with a travelling carnival. Paul Moritz finds them.

Henry tells Paul the reason for their flight is the Monster's demand that Henry create a Mate.

The Monster has followed Paul. He shadows the carnival caravan as it moves out of town, and while Henry sleeps, kills the horses which are pulling Henry's wagon, pulls the wagon off the road, then takes Henry to the edge of a waterfall.

Henry resists the Monster's unspoken demand that a Mate be created, until the Monster shows him, in the pool below the waterfall the face of a dead girl, and Henry realizes that Elizabeth is in danger.

He therefore sets up a laboratory in the carnival wagon, while the Monster garners bodies for him from various morgues, etc.

Using a high voltage line, Henry is on the point of complete success with his experiment when the line short circuits. The Monster takes his Mate away, but she doesn't live long. The Monster, in a rage, returns to the carnival, frees the animals, gets into a battle with a lion, and is finally killed, leaving Paul, Elizabeth, and Henry to live happily ever after.

Only point of similarity in this script is the Mate idea.

March 23, 1935
Finlay McDermid

THE RETURN OF FRANKENSTEIN

by

Philip MacDonald

Four years after the burning of the mill, Frankenstein is so engrossed in selling a powerful death ray to the League of Nations that he neglects his wife , Elizabeth, who is in a hospital. Victor Moritz is indignant with Henry, in love with Henry's wife.

Demonstration of the death ray blasts all life within radius of the beam, but restores life to the artificially created Monster, who climbs out of the mill wreckage and is drawn toward the laboratory.

1.   Indication that the Monster is not vicious until aroused is given when the Monster plays ball with Henry's two year old son. But Frankenstein realizes he must kill the creature.

The Monster endangers Elizabeth's life, and when Elizabeth regains consciousness, she calls for Victor instead of Henry. Henry, therefore, determines to do away with himself as well as the Monster.

The Monster blunders into the laboratory, turns on the death ray and the ray kills off whole cities' of people before Frankenstein succeeds in his plan of capturing his creature.

Bound in steel chains, the Monster faces the death ray. Not being able to move toward it, the Monster's life leaves its body by proxy (or something.) Henry moves into the ray, leaving Victor and Elizabeth free to marry each other...

1.   The only point which in any way resembles later scripts is this indication that the Monster likes companionship.....

UNIVERSAL PROPERTY   Finlay McDermid
First draft treatment   March 28, 1935
June 10, 1933

THE RETURN OF FRANKENSTEIN

by

Tom Reed

SUMMARY:

      Frankenstein, not badly injured from his fall from the mill, is helped into a carriage where his friend, Victor Moritz, is incredulous at Henry's confession that he created the Monster, now presumably dead in the mill.

      At the castle, Elizabeth and her younger sister, Karen, are relieved to greet their returning boy friends. The gruffly jovial Baron Frankenstein suggests that they go ahead with the wedding plans as soon as they can locate the Bishop, who is still in hiding.

*   The Monster, when the mill is in embers, slinks off into the forest. At a moon-lit pool, he stops to drink, sees his own reflection for the first time.

\#   He enters a peasant's hut, and the peasant disappears through the window. The Monster helps himself to food, goes to sleep. He has discovered in his pocket an envelope containing Frankenstein's notes, but can't read it. Three peasants return and rout the sleeping Monster, who kills one of them in his flight.

      A year later (presumably), Baron Frankenstein, his son and daughter-in-law, and Karen are visiting Victor Moritz' chateau. The Baron insists that the party return to the Frankenstein castle before Elizabeth's child is born. Everyone is very happy.

%   The Monster spies upon a peasant family, and learns to read, by watching the lessons received by an eight year old boy. The Monster also tries his voice. He performs various household tasks in gratitude. The blind grandfather accepts him as a friend, but the terrified father gets help to chase the Monster away.

      Frankenstein's boy is christened, and a hunting party is held in the mountains. While chasing a wolf, Frankenstein meets the Monster.

&   The Monster wants a Mate for himself. Unless Frankenstein will manufacture one for him, he will force Henry's hand. As a demonstration of what he has in mind, the Monster kills the Baron.

      At the news, Victor and Karen decide not to announce their engagement, as they had intended. Frankenstein, visited by the Monster, is given to understand that his own wife and child will be the next victims; he, therefore agrees to the Monster's demands.

      In a series of morgue robberies, snatching of bodies from the scenes of accidents, etc., Frankenstein collects his raw materials.
\$ (A railroad accident and other modern indications are used.)

      Elizabeth is worried as her husband shows signs of madness, goes frequently to his hidden laboratory in the mountains. Victor, surmising the truth, attempts to follow Henry and the dwarf on the night when an electrical storm, for which Henry has been waiting, is raging outside. Victor loses his way.

The Monster arrives, as the experiments seemingly fails. Henry says he can't snatch any more bodies, that the Monster will have to supply them if he wants Henry to succeed in a second attempt. The Monster goes to the castle, where Elizabeth manages to hide the baby, but is killed, herself.

@ Victor finally finds the laboratory, is horrified to find what Henry is attempting. But when he hears Henry's story, he comforts him, urges him to leave the country. There are signs of life in the Mate.

The Monster returns with Elizabeth's body, sees his Mate move, and goes to the operating table.

/ Frankenstein, seeing an opportunity to kill both the creatures, turns on the high powered voltage which instantly kills the Mate. The Monster, seizes Henry and drags him into the electrical path.

Victor returns to Karen and Frankenstein's son.......

FOOTNOTES

* The reflection in the pool is utilized in both shooting and Balderston scripts.

The envelope containing notes on Frankenstein's experiment is similar to the notebook used in Balderston script.

¢ This scene is decidedly like the educational system used in Balderston script. The blind friend is used in both Balderston and shooting scripts.

& The Mate. The one suggested by Reed is to be a creature as horrible as is the Monster itself. The mountain setting for the Monster's blackmailing demand on Henry is similar to the setting for the kidnapping suggested by Balderston.

$ Use of modern inventions. In shooting script, Mrs. Shelley's lines in the prologue provide an excuse for this jump into the future, however.

@ Victor Moritz is briefly used to reflect the religious horror at Henry's experiments. In Balderston script, Father Gerard plays this element up still more.

/ The death means used in shooting script, although in the latter, the current is turned on by the Monster.

THE RETURN OF FRANKENSTEIN

by

Tom Reed

JUNE 29, 1933

A screenplay elaboration of First draft treatment. Victor Moritz' name changed to Paul, comedy between Bishop and Baron played up. No essential plot difference.

JULY 14, 1933

Minor changes in continuity, dialogue, etc. No plot change.

JULY 25, FINAL REED VERSION

1.   Includes addition of a scene in which Bertha (character substituted for eight-year old grandson of the blind man) goes swimming in a lake. Monster watches her, with pleasure, but when he attracts her attention, the girl, in panic, gets into deep water, drowns. The Monster carries her body back to the blind man, and sorrowfully goes, of his own accord, away from his friend's house.

2.   There is a brief scene in a confessional, in which Henry attempts to gain absolution, but he cannot bring himself to confess that he has created a Man.

NOTES

1.   Somewhat similar to the rescue scene used in early Balderston script and in shooting script.

2.   Suggestion of religious motif which Balderston greatly developed......

Finlay McDermid
March 28, 1935

THE RETURN OF FRANKENSTEIN

by

William Hurlbut

October 30, 1934. First Hurlbut adaptation.

Substantially the same as shooting script. Father Gerard
figures briefly in the final sequence, to rebuke Frankenstein for
his sin. But the final catastrophe is caused by the Monster
accidentally shortcircuiting the electric current. Pretorius
scenes are all incorporated, but show minor differences from final
script.

Ad restoration by Al Magliochetti

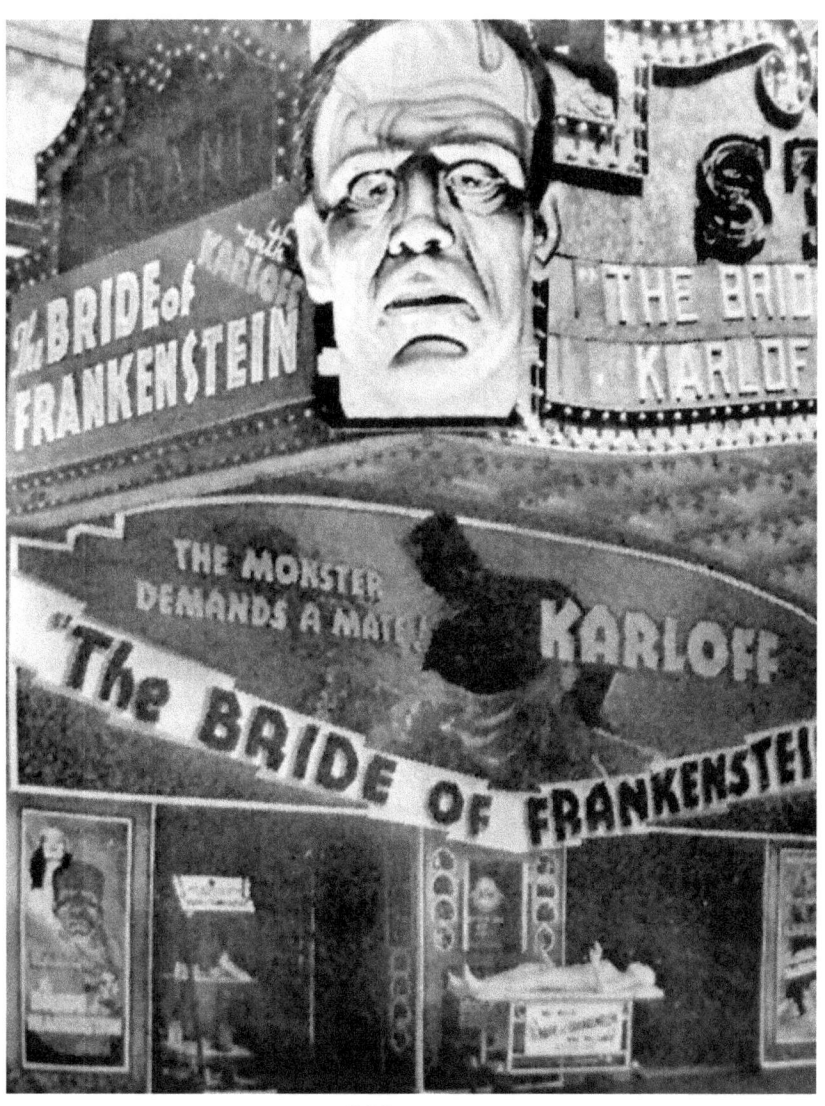

www.ingramcontent.com/pod-product-compliance
Lightning Source LLC
Chambersburg PA
CBHW080012040726
47505CB00016B/2247